The Sign Around My Neck

Lucas Hasten

Summary: Eleven-year-old Lu (short for "Lucy")
has grown up surrounded by friends and family
who think of him as a girl, but he has a secret that
he has only begun to share with himself: Inside, he
has always been a boy.

[1. Transgender people – Fiction. 2. Gender
identity – Fiction. 3. Identity – Fiction. 4. Self-
acceptance – Fiction. 5. Schools – Fiction. 6.
Middle schools – Fiction. 7. Family life – Fiction.]

For Tess, without whom this book would never have been written.

1

My stomach is growling so loudly that the whole class can hear it. Maddie giggles as she jabs me with an organic granola bar, but it's goji berries and chia seeds so I tell her no thanks, that stuff is like chewing on pebbles and grass. It's almost lunchtime anyway and I'm not that desperate, even though I don't get much of a breakfast anymore since Mom started working. I miss having pancakes in the middle of the week, smothered in butter and drowning in syrup. That only happens on weekends now.

"All right, everyone. Time to clean up for lunch!" Mrs. Rubin stands at the front of the classroom, clapping her hands to get our attention.

Maddie looks at me, dramatically holding her head in her hands. "Finally! Your stomach is hurting my ears."

I stick my tongue out at her and start putting the covers back on the jars of paint we've been using. Ever since March, we've been spending almost half of our time working on the fifth grade play. It's the most fun I've ever had in school, plus, we're learning a lot. Our music teacher, Ms. Baxter, helped us to come up with the idea for the script. We're telling a story about two kids who get locked in a costume shop where the mannequins come to life after dark. Each one is wearing an outfit that represents a part of the 20th century – Ms. Baxter said that means the 1900s – and they teach the kids about what happened in America during that time.

Today we're painting a backdrop for a scene about the 1920s, when there was something called

"Prohibition." Drinking alcohol was against the law then. No wine, no beer, or anything. It wasn't a very good law, though, because people still wanted to drink, so they did it anyway. They bought liquor that came from criminals who'd do anything to make money. There were even shoot-outs and murders. The backdrop is the inside of a speakeasy, which was a secret nightclub where people met to drink when it was still illegal. I'm painting tables and chairs.

I head for the sink to wash my paintbrushes as the class begins lining up at the door, girls on the right and boys on the left. I'm watching the water run over them, blending the blue we used for the walls with the red we used for the chairs and flowing purple into the drain when suddenly, time stops. Aware that something has just happened, my brain lets it seep in slowly, the way it takes my hands a while to get cold inside my gloves when it's freezing outside. Little by little, the information fades into focus until finally I realize: Jake Ruggiero has just kissed me!

It doesn't make any sense. He doesn't even like me! He's the cutest boy in the class, and *none* of them like me that way. They think I'm ugly. I know this for a fact because I was dumb enough to ask some of them to sign my yearbook, and they wrote mean things, like: "To a girl who's really built . . . like a Mack truck!" and "Roses are red/violets are blue/gorillas are ugly/and so is Lu!"

Still, he snuck up on me when my head was down and kissed me on the cheek, totally out of nowhere. Maybe he *does* like me. How is that even possible? No boy has ever kissed me before. Everyone thinks he's gorgeous, so I should be happy – shouldn't I? All of these thoughts run through my head in a split second because it's only an instant before Jake turns back to the class and says, "Okay, I did it! Now where's my five bucks?"

My heart starts beating so hard that it's all I can hear. Part of me wants to run away and part of me wants to scream, so I clench my teeth instead and focus on washing my brushes. The kids are halfway out the door, but whoever's there is either howling with laughter or shocked. Maddie is just a few feet away from me, staring down at the floor. She's not laughing, but she won't look me in the eye. Ignoring them all, I finish up and follow the line out to the lunchroom. My face is hot, and my head feels like it's full of fuzzy wool – I can't think and don't want to.

In the lunchroom, I take my usual seat next to Maddie and pull out my lunch bag. I keep my eyes fixed firmly on my food because I don't want to look anyone in the face. Mom's decided that she and I should both be on a diet, so she's packed me some dried-out leftover chicken, a few carrots, an apple, and a bottle of water. Note to Mom: There's no fun in this lunch! There's salad dressing, but it tastes like vinegar so I skip it, looking with longing across the table at everyone else's food. Maddie's the opposite of me and way too skinny. She's chowing down on a PB&J with chocolate milk and chocolate chip cookies. I'm too angry, too embarrassed, or too numb to cry. Probably all three.

No one mentions the kiss. Maybe Jake is laughing his head off about it with the guys over at his table, but *my* friends are acting like it never happened. Maddie's talking about auditions for the play with Michael and Ben, while Valentina and Asher are going over plans for their gymnastics meet this weekend. I'm not saying anything and I'm not eating either, just pushing the chicken cubes around inside the plastic box with the fork I brought from home. Everybody's too busy talking to notice.

2

I don't want to go to school. I want to lie in bed and feel bad for a while. I'm not going to tell Mom what happened yesterday, and besides, she wouldn't let me stay home, anyway. Now that she has to go to work, I have to go to school unless I have a fever. But I just can't do it today.

I bury myself under the covers, face and all, and lie there thinking about it for a while. Finally, I get up, switch on the lamp next to my bed, and go out to the bathroom to get the thermometer. Poking my head into my parents' bedroom, I see Mom putting on her makeup. Dad's already left for work. "Mom," I say, in my best sick voice, "I don't feel well. I think I have a fever."

"Go check it," she says, not looking away from her mirror. Her long, blonde hair is pulled back into a ponytail, and her eyes are open extra wide as she puts on her mascara. I think she's beautiful without any make-up, but she jokes that she's afraid she'll lose in court without it. "Juries like good-looking lawyers," she says with a wink, but I get the feeling it's true.

Back in my bedroom, I carefully touch the tip of the thermometer to the lightbulb over and over again, just a second or two each time, so that it starts to get hot. I've done this only twice before when I felt too sad to go to school, so I know to be careful about it. Little by little, the temperature rises to 100.2 degrees. I don't want to overdo it because Mom might take me to the doctor, who'll know I'm faking.

I get back into bed, completely under the covers again, until I hear Mom's footsteps in the hall and poke my head out. When she walks in, the ponytail is gone, and her hair spills across her shoulders.

"So? What's the story?"

I hand her the thermometer, trying to look as sick as possible. "I have a headache and my throat hurts." It's easy enough to lie in the moment, but it always feels bad afterwards.

"Well," she sighs, "it's over a hundred so you're staying home." She puts her hand on my forehead and it feels so good to be touched that I wish she would scoop me up in her arms and hold me for the rest of the day. "You do feel warm." She leaves the room with an "I'll be back," and I take a deep breath, relieved not to have to face anyone at school today.

Still in bed, I reach for my phone and hit the power button. I wonder if anyone has said anything online about what happened yesterday. It doesn't matter. Everyone already knows. The phone turns on, blinking lights and logos, and my notifications start coming in. I send "Happy birthday!" messages to the people whose names pop up, trying to write something personal to each one, and then I start looking at Valentina's photos before Mom comes back down the hall. I slip my phone under the covers.

She walks in and sets a tray with tea, toast, and a glass of water down on my desk. The tea has honey and lemon in it and the toast has strawberry jam. I haven't had bread in a while so I'm extra happy to see it. It smells delicious.

"Eat this so I can give you something for your fever." She points to a pill on the tray. "And take this when you're done." I'm not really sick, so I'll put it back in the bottle when she's gone.

She comes over and sits down on the bed next to me. "Okay, now. I'm in court today, so you're on your own. Leave the door locked and don't answer it if anybody comes. You know the rules, right?"

"Right." I have them memorized because we've done this before. "Don't answer the phone unless it's someone I know. Don't turn on the oven or the stove. Don't use the fireplace." Mom is nodding, unsmiling, as I go through the list, trying to keep doing my sick voice. "Don't call you or Dad unless it's an emergency.

10

Don't invite anyone over. Don't leave the house. Don't go skydiving. Don't fall asleep on the beach. Don't walk behind a horse. Don't let your right hand know what your left hand is doing."

"What?" Mom finally breaks into a laugh with a snort. "All right, all right, wise guy. You're pretty funny for a sick kid." She kisses my forehead and stands up. "I have to go. Be a good girl. I'll see you at 4 o'clock."

"Love you, Mom."

"I love you too, Lu." She only calls me Lucy when she's angry, which is great, because I don't like it. It's a pretty name, but it's not *me*.

Mom leaves and I wait until I hear her start the car and drive away before throwing off the covers. The first thing I do is run quietly to my parents' bedroom, whose window looks out over the driveway, just to make sure that she's gone.

Happy to be on my own, I go back to my room and sit at my desk, sipping the tea and nibbling at the toast as slowly as I can, trying to make it last as long as possible. I'm not sure why Mom thinks I need to lose weight. It's probably because she thinks she's fat and she's worried about me being fat, too. I think she looks great, though, and even though I'm big for a girl, I look normal if you compare me to the boys.

Life would be so much easier if I were a boy. Nobody would think I'm fat, for one thing. The guys wouldn't make fun of me for looking like a dude because I'd *be* one. Not that it would be so great because a lot of them are jerks, but still, some of them are nice, like Ben, and Asher, and Michael. I'd be one of the good ones. And they wouldn't expect me to want to hold their hands or think they're cool, or anything. I could just be myself.

I'm different and I have to hide it because if people knew, they would think less of me. Even my parents. I figured it out one day when I was four years old because I came down from my bedroom and walked into the living room wearing nothing but a pair of shorts. Dad was sitting there dressed exactly the same way; he looked up from his book at me with a raised eyebrow. Mom took me by the hand and led me back to the stairs.

"Go to your room and put on a blouse."

"Why?" I whined. "Dad doesn't have to!"

"Because he's a boy, and you're a girl, and that's the way it is."

"Oh," I thought. I didn't say it, but that's what I thought. Just, "Oh." I went back upstairs and did as I was told.

I love my Mom. I want to be good. I just don't want to be a girl.

3

My phone is ringing. It's Dad, so I answer it in my sick voice.

"What's wrong, baby? Mom told me you were feeling sick. Are you okay? Do you need me to come home?" Dad's like that. He'd be happy to leave work to come home and take care of me if I asked him to, even if he'd be missing something important. Nothing means more to him than me and Mom.

"No, I'm okay. Just a sore throat and a headache. I'm really sleepy, too," I add, hoping he'll let me off the phone.

"Well, call me if you need me, okay? Make sure you drink a lot of water."

14

"Okay, Dad, I will. I love you."

"Love you too, honey."

I hang up before he can add anything and put my head down on my desk. I feel sad and guilty for staying home from school and pretending to be sick. But I feel even worse when I think about going back. Mostly it's Sam and Noah I don't want to see. Jake's never been mean to me before, but those two almost always are. It's like I'm walking around with a big, red X on my forehead that tells certain people to make fun of me.

My phone buzzes; it's a message from Maddie.

"Where are you? Why aren't you here?" It must be lunchtime or her phone would be turned off and laying in the bottom of her backpack.

"Because I'm sick." I have to tell everyone the same story or I'll forget what it is. "I have a headache and a sore throat and a little fever. ☹"

"Oh no! Feel better! Talk later?"

"Sure."

"Okay! ♥♥♥."

"."

It's weird that she hasn't said anything about Jake kissing me yet. She's my best friend, and she's being super quiet, which isn't like her. Usually I can't get her to shut up. She'll go on and on about her little dog, or the latest annoying thing her sister did, or how she's training for a marathon, and even though she's being serious, she's also cracking jokes the whole time. Her favorite thing to do is to say something hysterical while I'm drinking, so I'll laugh and shoot water out of my nose. It hurts like crazy, even though it *is* funny. One time she did it while I was eating jelly beans, and her mom almost had to take me to the hospital, so she's supposedly not allowed to do it anymore. It doesn't stop her, although she does stick to liquids now.

Maddie's the opposite of me in a lot of ways. She's thin and athletic, while I'm average and geeky. She beats me at every sport, but I still have fun playing with her. It's probably because she's always laughing and being silly, and when she wins she never makes me feel bad about it. She just looks at me with those

16

mischievous brown eyes and says something that cracks me up. Every time. She's the only person I show my poems to because no matter what, she always loves them. She makes me feel like I'm good at something.

I've been lying in bed, reading, but I get up and close my door so I can look at myself in the full-length mirror that hangs on it. I take off my pajama top and examine my chest. It's not exactly flat anymore, but I don't have nearly as much there as some of the girls. Please, please, please, I hope I never do. My hair, which used to be blonde like Mom's but turned brown in the first grade, is longer than I want it to be. It's all one length and comes straight down to my shoulders. I push it back behind my ears and pull it all together into a rubber band, pretending it's short. I look closely at my face. If I cut my hair, would it look more like a boy's face?

I walk barefoot down the hall to the bathroom. My father's shaving cream and razor are there on the counter where he always leaves them. It feels like I'm doing something wrong, but I don't care. I want to see

17

what it's like. I reach for the can of shaving cream and spray some on my hand. I love the touch of it on my skin, soft and firm at the same time, smooth and cool. Looking in the mirror, I spread it across my face the way I've seen Dad do it many times: From my cheeks to my chin and partway down my neck, with a little bit above my upper lip. It looks like I've got a white beard. Maybe one day.

Carefully, I run the razor across my face the way Dad does, starting with my cheek and shaving down. It feels so right and so exciting, but also like something I'd better not get caught doing. I cut myself a tiny bit near my nose, and it's bleeding, but it doesn't hurt at all. I press a tiny piece of a tissue to it so it sticks there. When I pull it off later, the bleeding will have stopped – a trick of Dad's. I finish and clean up after myself, being careful not to leave any signs of what I've been doing. When I'm done, I try to pee into the toilet while I'm standing up, but that almost makes a giant mess so I give up and sit down to finish.

Back in my room, I pull out the script for the play. Once we all agreed on the story, the kids in Ms. Baxter's music class wrote the lines. It's a musical, so there are a bunch of songs, too. Ms. Baxter taught us real songs from each period, and we wrote new words for them. I write poetry all the time, and I'm great at making up rhymes, so after a couple of classes, everyone started looking at me when they were stuck for a word. "Come on, Lu," they'd say, "think of something!" and I'd wind up changing the line so it made more sense and rhymed in an unexpected way. Everyone else was always rhyming "me" with "see" and "you" with "true," but I tried to be cleverer. One day I rhymed "fought for you" with "World War Two," and a couple of kids literally patted me on the back.

I'm excited for try-outs. I've been in the school band since third grade, and I've even had solos on my saxophone, so I'm not afraid to be on stage. I don't want to play any of the girl's parts, and there's no way I'm trying out for a boy's part, so I go through the script and circle the parts that don't have to be one or the other. There are a lot of them: There's a bartender in the 1920s scene, a bandleader in the 1940s scene, a group of protestors in the 1960s scene, a DJ in the 1980s scene, and at least five others. I'm glad I have so many choices.

4

I'm settled under a blanket on the couch, watching a video from my Dad's collection of old movie musicals. He likes to watch them on Superbowl Sunday and days like that as his way of defiantly not watching football, which he says is too "hyper-macho" for him. I've got a cup of tea next to me on the coffee table and a bowl of microwave popcorn on my lap. My cell phone is on the nightstand upstairs in my bedroom because I'm not in the mood to talk to anyone. If I have it with me, I'll be too tempted to check my notifications and "like" stuff, and then people will see I'm online and start chatting me.

The movie is called *Singin' in the Rain*, and Dad says it's a "classic," by which he means that people his age love it and nobody my age has heard of it. It stars a dancer named Gene Kelly who was famous in the 1950s. The music is different from what I'm normally into, but it's not bad. The people sing so clearly that I can understand every word, but in a very plain style, not at all like singers nowadays who do all kinds of cool things with their voices. The rhythms could be pretty awesome, though. Sometimes one reminds me of a song on my playlist – except it came first, maybe sixty years earlier. Even some of the dance moves look just like the ones I've seen in music videos online. There are lots of differences, for sure, but the basic ideas are there.

One thing that sticks out to me every time I watch old movies with Dad is how nice the men are to the women. They open doors for them to walk through, hold umbrellas over their heads in the rain, and pull chairs for them to sit on out from under dining tables. Dad says they were "practicing the art of chivalry." He told me that back then, people didn't give women much credit for being able to take care of themselves. They thought women were weak, so men had to do all those things for them. Now that we know women are equals to men, chivalry isn't in style any more. I understand why, but I think it's sad. I can't help thinking that I'd like to be the kind of man who holds the door open for the woman I'm with. Or even for the next guy.

The house phone rings and I check the caller ID before hitting the pause button to answer it.

"Hi, Cam," I say, going with my sick voice.

"Hey, you're not answering texts. What's up? Mom said you were sick."

"Geez, news travels fast."

"Of course. You know they had their daily briefing." Cameron's talking about his mom and mine, who've been best friends since dinosaur times. They talk every morning from their cars while they both drive to work. His mom is basically my aunt, and he's kind of my cousin. He's four years older than me, but it's never mattered. "Cam" was the first name I learned, right after Mom and Dad. He was a very persistent five-year-old, though, repeating it over and over until I finally said it back to him.

"Yeah," I say, "I'm a little sick. What about you? What are you doing home?"

"I pulled the thermometer trick."

It's all I can do to keep from laughing out loud about the coincidence, but I don't want to give myself away. Plus, I know he's got a good reason.

"Why? Are you okay?"

"Yeah. I just couldn't handle P.E. today. Not after last time."

"I wouldn't have gone either, Cam. I don't understand why they make us play dodgeball. It's not right. It's like they *want* to give the jocks a chance to beat up on the rest of us."

"Yeah, well, you're lucky you don't have any junk for anybody to aim at. I can't tell you how much that hurts. That ball is really hard."

"I know. I'm sorry." I really am, too, because I saw the pain on his face that day. Also, because – as he pointed out – I don't have any "junk."

"I can't go back there, Lu. I just can't." I don't say anything, and after a long time he adds, "I'll never let them get me in that locker room again." He didn't tell me what happened there, which is how I know it must have been really bad.

"I know," I say, "I get it. Did you talk to Aunt Caroline?"

"No! Are you kidding? She's way too emotional right now. She doesn't need this on top of everything else."

"What are you going to do? You can't heat up the thermometer every day."

"I don't know. I'll figure it out."

"Shouldn't you tell someone? At school, maybe?"

"Are you kidding? That'll only make it worse, once they know I ratted on them."

"Well, you have to do something, Cam. You're going to get hurt again."

25

"I know."

"Maybe I should talk to -"

"No! Don't say anything to anyone. I swear, Lu, if you do, I'll never talk to you again." He sounds panicked.

"All right, all right! Don't worry. It's cool. I won't say anything."

"You'd better not." His voice relaxes. "I'd hate to have to give up my chess partner."

"Only because I'm not good enough to beat you!" I'm expecting a laugh but it doesn't come.

"You will be," he says. "Talk to you later."

We hang up, and I press play, but it takes me a long time to start paying attention to the movie because I'm still thinking about Cameron. I don't understand why Aunt Caroline hasn't seen through him yet. I mean, he keeps showing up with bruises and excuses. I'd talk to Mom about it but I don't want to risk his friendship by going behind his back when he's probably right about it only making things worse.

The movie pulls me back in when the scene with
the song from the title comes on – the one where Gene
Kelly dances through an empty city street, singing his
heart out in a downpour. I love the look of joy on his
face as he sings about how happy he feels, now that
he's fallen in love. I can see myself in his soaking wet
suit and hat, tap-dancing my way along a watery
sidewalk without a care for my clothes as I allow the
warmth of some future romance to flow over me, a
man in love with a woman. A short time later, I hear
Mom unlock the front door.

"Hi, honey!" She walks in, drops her keys and
handbag on the table, and comes straight at me to place
her hand on my forehead. "How are you feeling?"

"Better," I say, hitting the pause button again and
trying to sound a bit less sick than I did this morning. I
don't want to stay home tomorrow and feel bad about
missing school again.

"Your fever's gone, that's for sure." She bends
down to give me a kiss. "That popcorn doesn't hurt
your throat?" she asks, nodding her head toward it.

27

"Not any more than the toast did." I know she thinks popcorn is a good snack because it doesn't have a lot of calories without any butter on it.

"Well okay, then. What happened to your face there?" She's got my chin in her hand and she's looking right at the cut under my nose. Mom doesn't miss a thing.

"I had an itch and I scratched myself by accident," I say, thinking fast.

Mom shakes her head at me. "You need to stop biting those nails of yours, Lu. Let them grow out and I'll give you a beautiful manicure!"

"You know I'm not into that, Mom."

"Who knows? Maybe one day you will be," she says with a smile. "I'm making you chicken soup for dinner. We'll knock whatever that bug is right out of you!" Mom hangs up her coat and heads into the kitchen to unpack the groceries and start cooking.

I hit "play" and get back to watching the movie. I love Gene Kelly. He's handsome and romantic, and he sings and dances in all kinds of styles, and he's *still* a man. I don't think a boy who dances like him would be very popular at my school. The guys make fun of any boy who does anything they think girls should do. It's funny. Now that women have equal rights to men, shouldn't men have equal rights to women?

5

Dad's working late tonight, so Mom and I have dinner together without him. She says he'll heat up the soup when he gets home. It's hard for me to keep pretending that I feel a little sick, but I don't want to blow my cover.

"Did you get your homework?"

"Yes. Mrs. Rubin emailed it to me. I'm in the middle of it."

"Good. You can finish it after dinner and when you're done and ready for bed, we can watch a movie together for a little while. Do you feel up to going to school tomorrow?"

"I think so. I'm better now and I'll probably be even better tomorrow."

"What's your homework about?"

"We're reading a book on the 'Westward Expansion'."

"What's that?" Mom says we study different things than they did when she was a kid, so sometimes she doesn't know what I'm talking about.

"It's how the colonists spread out from the East to the West and settled the whole country."

"Mm hmm," she says, chewing, which means she wants me to keep talking.

"I guess it was hard. Exploring new places that weren't on maps yet. Wagon trains crossing canyons and stuff."

"You sound pretty bored by it."

"Well, no. I mean, it's just . . . it's all 'mountain men' and Lewis and Clark. All the heroes are guys. I'd be pretty unhappy if I lived then."

"What about Sacagawea? The woman who was their guide? Wasn't she a hero?" I guess Mom does know something about this, after all.

"Well sure," I admit, "but she was Native American, and she was actually enslaved by a White man who made the entire trip with them. He owned her like property."

"Oh, my. I had no idea."

"Yeah."

"Well, that's awful." She frowns and thinks for a minute. "Women contributed a lot, you know, even if they weren't out cutting their way through the forest like Lewis and Clark."

"I know, I know," I say, because I want her to stop talking about it. Sure, women helped out, but not in any of the ways that I'd want to. I excuse myself from the table and take my dishes to the sink. They had babies, I think to myself. That's not something I'll ever do.

I go upstairs to my room and check my phone for the first time in hours. I've got six messages from

Maddie, two from Ben, and one from Asher. I start
with Asher because he messaged me first: He's asking
if I still want come see him and Valentina compete at
their gymnastics meet on Saturday. I go into the
hallway and yell down from the top of the stairs,
"Mom!" She comes to the bottom and looks up at me.

"*Vas vilstu*?" It means, "What do you want?" in
Yiddish, but it's not as harsh as that. When she says it
to me, it's more like "What can I do for you?"

"Can I go to Asher and Valentina's meet on
Saturday? Asher's dad is driving."

"When will you be back?"

"I don't know. It's in the morning."

"All right. Just make sure that I have Asher's
father's phone number."

"Okay, thanks!" I message Asher and tell him yes.

Ben is asking if I've seen that new horror movie yet,
and if I want to go with him. We've been talking about
it for weeks. I tell him my Dad already said he can take
us on Sunday, and Ben says cool, he'll check with his
parents.

33

Maddie wants to know if I'm feeling better and if I'm coming to school tomorrow. That's the first message. The other five are about taking her dog to the vet this afternoon, and I'm seriously worried as I read them because I love Princess, but it turns out that she's fine after all. I message Maddie back and let her know that I'm happy Princess is okay, and to please give her a kiss for me, and I'll see her at school tomorrow. She starts to get into another story, but I say I'm sleepy and I need to do my homework and go to bed. Honestly, I'd rather watch a movie with Mom tonight than be on my phone.

I finish my homework, shower and brush my teeth, and put on a clean pair of pajamas. While I do that, Mom changes the sheets on my bed so I don't have to sleep on "last night's germs." Clean sheets always feel so nice, but I'm sorry she went to the trouble. I know she's tired.

We go downstairs to the couch, and I lie down with my head on her lap, facing the TV. Mom hits "play" and restarts the movie I was watching.

"We don't have to watch this," I tell her. "I'm already in the middle of it."

"Are you kidding? *Singin' in the Rain*? That's one of my all-time favorites! I adore Gene Kelly. I know all of the words to all of the songs."

We watch the rest of the movie and Mom sings along to a lot of it, trying not to annoy me. I tell her it's fine, I don't mind. I love it that my Mom is sitting here with me, singing these old songs with her hand on my head. It feels like my own mini-musical.

"He's such a good-looking man," she says at one point. "They don't make 'em like that anymore. Except for your father, of course."

"I know what you mean," I say, because I do. She thinks he's cute in a way that means she'd like to be with him, but I think he's cute in a way that means I'd like to *be* him.

6

We're having try-outs today for the play, and I'm too excited to concentrate on anything else. I know all the lines by heart because I helped to write them. I'm sure I'll get a part, probably more than one, because there are so many of them, and not every kid even wants to be in the play. Asher and Valentina are busy with gymnastics, and Ben's going to his cousin's wedding in Chicago the day before the performance.

The morning is dragging on, mostly because I'm just waiting for it to end, but also because we're doing fractions, which I hate. Why can't I just use the calculator on my phone? I mean, it's the 21st century, isn't it? I'm thinking about this instead of working on

36

the problem in front of me when I see, out of the corner of my eye, Asher get up to go sharpen his pencil and trip over something. He doesn't just fall because please, the guy's an incredible gymnast, but his face turns bright red and he looks a little shaken. I'm wondering what he stumbled over when I notice that Sam is sitting right where Asher tripped with his foot sticking out into the aisle, looking pleased with himself. He and Noah are both holding back laughter. I'm glad Asher didn't give them the satisfaction of falling, but part of me wants to go over there and punch Sam in the face. I know it's not right, but I bet it would feel great!

After lunch, those of us who want to try out for the play are sent to the multi-purpose room. Groups of us start practicing lines together while Ms. Baxter calls us over, one at a time, to read for her. Maddie, Michael, and I are reading the scene that takes place during the 1960s. We take turns saying the lines of the different protesters who are marching for civil rights. Then we do a chant where I lead the call and they do the response:

"What do we want?"

"Freedom!"

"When do we want it?"

"Now!"

"That's pretty cool," says Maddie.

"Yes it is," says Michael. "My people!" He pumps his fist in the air and then doubles over with laughter. I'm glad he thinks it's funny because I think it's awful that African Americans had to fight for their rights. Michael's no different from me; in fact, he's a lot smarter than I am.

When it's my turn to try out for Ms. Baxter, I read the lines for five different parts that could be played by either boys or girls. The point is, she won't make me wear a dress if I get any of them. She seems happy with me when I go back to my friends. Once Maddie has her turn, we're all done, so we sit and watch the rest of the try-outs.

Lots of the girls want the role of the mom in the scene about the 1960s. She's telling her kids about the Reverend Dr. Martin Luther King, Jr., who led peaceful protests to show America how wrong it was to treat people differently just because of the color of their skin. It's an important time in history, but we wrote the scene to be funny so the little kids would stay interested. The girls are all being so serious, though, and I'm getting frustrated. They're ruining the best lines.

My friend, Mia, is up next, so I decide to coach her. "Did you ever see that old TV show, *The Babysitter*? The one with the woman who has that funny voice?" Mia shakes her head at me. "She has a major New York accent, like this," I say, and I read a few of the lines in a way that makes them sound like they're coming out of my nose.

"Who's that?" I turn my head and Ms. Baxter is looking right at me. "Was that you, Lu?"

"Yes," I answer, hoping she's not angry with me.

"That's perfect!" she cries. "That's it, you're playing the part!" I can tell by her tone that she's thrilled.

Michael and Maddie look at me like I've just won a ticket to Disneyland and start high-fiving and fist bumping me. There's a rock in my throat and a hole in my stomach, and all I can think about is the dress I'll have to wear.

7

"Of course you should bring him! Tell him I'm cooking vegetarian tonight and I'll be disappointed if he's not here to help me with the eggplant. I never have any idea what to do with it." Mom's on the phone with Aunt Caroline, and I can only hear her half of the conversation. They must be talking about Cameron.

"I know. I know," says Mom. "It's been hard on him. Did his father really have to move so far away?" Cam's parents got divorced last year, and his dad moved to England for a new job. He's been sad for a long time, but not about that. He says his dad never paid any attention to him before the divorce, so there isn't much to miss about him now.

41

"Look, it's Friday night. Pull him up off the couch and get yourselves over here. And do me a favor and pick up some French bread on your way, okay? Great! See you soon." Mom hangs up the phone and turns to me.

"I'm making moussaka." She shrugs. "I have no idea what to do without Cameron."

"Order pizza?" I ask, a little too hopefully.

"Ha, ha. You like moussaka, don't you?"

"I don't know. Is that the one with the potatoes?"

"No," she says, pulling onions and garlic out of the pantry. "It's like a Greek lasagna, only it's layers of baked eggplant with ground meat and feta cheese. We usually do it vegetarian, though, with mushrooms instead of meat. It's Cameron's favorite."

"Oh yeah! I *love* that!"

"I thought so. Do you want to help?"

"Sure," I say, and she hands me the garlic to peel. "So what's going on with him? Is he okay?"

"I don't know. Aunt Caroline says he's been depressed." Mom sets a heavy cast iron pan on the

42

stovetop with a *CLANK!* and lights a small candle next to the cutting board, which means she's about to dice the onion. The flame is supposed to burn off the chemical that makes your eyes water. "Did he say anything to you the last time he was here?"

"No," I answer quickly, even though he did.

"You two spent a lot of time together. What did you talk about?" She's dicing the onion and dropping it from the flat side of her knife into the butter and olive oil sizzling in the pan.

"I don't know. Nothing really. We just played chess." I'm lying of course, because I'd never betray his trust. We talked about him getting pushed around because he's different. He's too proud and embarrassed to tell his mom about it, so he makes up a story every time he gets hurt and sweeps it all away.

"That's really sweet of him to teach you to play."

"Yeah. He's so nice about it, too. He tries to let me win, but I'm still really bad at it so he can't help but beat me. He apologizes when he captures my pieces. It's pretty funny. We laugh about it."

43

Mom finishes with the onion and gets to work cleaning mushrooms. When I'm done with the garlic, she puts me on the job, too, because there are a lot of them. We use a dry piece of paper towel to carefully wipe the dirt off the cap of each one because you're not supposed to get them wet before you cook them. It makes them slimy and soggy.

"Aunt Caroline is worried about him," she says, skillfully dusting her mushrooms while I struggle not to break mine. "She says he doesn't have any friends."

"That's not true!" I argue. "He has lots of friends. From all over the world."

"What do you mean? Online?"

"Yeah. He's always chatting with someone."

"Are any of these people real?"

"Mom! Of course they're real!"

"Lu, having friends online is not a substitute for being with real people, face-to-face." She leaves the rest of the mushrooms to me and starts pulling spices out of the cabinets to measure into little bowls.

"I know that. But sometimes people are nicer to you online. At least there, you get to choose who you hang out with."

"There's a lot of bullying online too, though, isn't there?"

"I guess so. But not in chat groups, where you have to be a member. There are all kinds of cool people in there with the same interests as you."

"I see," she nods. "Still, everyone needs to get out once in a while."

"Yeah," I say, thinking about chess. Cameron's been teaching me because Mom's right: He needs someone else to play with. It's true that all his friends are people he only knows online. That's because when you write back and forth with someone, you actually read what they're saying and make up your mind about them based on that. But when you meet someone in person, you judge them right away based on how they look or what they're wearing. For some people, Cam comes off better in writing.

Part of the problem is that he doesn't fit in where he is. All anybody cares about there is sports because they're state champions, and if a guy's not on one team or another, he gets pushed around like garbage. Cam's nerdy and artistic in a way that makes him stand out, and now he's a target. Someone gave him a black eye once, just for wearing nail polish. I couldn't believe anybody would actually punch a person for that. A few days later I heard Mom and Aunt Caroline talking about it and realized Cam had told his mom he'd done it to himself by accident.

It's not long before they both come through the door with their arms full of grocery bags. "What in the world?" says Mom. "I only asked for French bread!"

"I know." Aunt Caroline sets her bags down, kissing me hello, while Cameron gives me a smile and immediately starts unpacking. "I set him loose and let him get whatever he wanted. Apparently, we're having pretzel s'mores and sundaes for dessert." It's obvious now that he's pulling everything out of the bags because he's digging for the two gallons of ice cream at the bottom so he can get them into the freezer before they melt.

"Caroline!" Mom frowns, not too upset, and then looks at me in surrender. This isn't something she'd normally let me do, but she knows I'm thrilled so she drops it.

"It was the only way I could get him off the couch," shrugs Aunt Caroline, and Cam hits me with a fist bump.

8

Asher and his dad pick me up early Saturday morning. He's got a grin on his face a mile wide because they're in his dad's '65 Mustang convertible, which is just about all he talks about besides gymnastics. He says he's going to inherit it one day and when he does, he'll be the dude with the hottest car in town, like it's going to make him popular all of a sudden. I hope so, because I know he could use a little help. Asher's a great guy and a terrific athlete, but you'd never know it to look at him. He's small for his age and his arms and legs are so skinny that he looks like a stick figure in a t-shirt and shorts. His blonde hair is so light that you almost can't see his eyebrows, and his skin is just about the color of milk. When you see him from a distance, the only thing that stands out, just barely, are his pale blue eyes.

I'm not sure why Sam and Noah give him such a hard time. They call him "gay" like it's an insult, when everybody knows that gay people are just like everyone else. It doesn't even make sense because Asher likes girls! It's just a stupid thing to say. It's probably because of the gymnastics, and because he's so small. They call him "fairy dancer" and "fairy queen." Sometimes they push him around on the playground, and I get angry at them and upset with myself. I want to make them stop but I'm afraid to risk having Sam and Noah to pay any more attention to me than they already do.

"Good morning, Lu!" Asher's dad hops out of the car to let me into the backseat. It's *huge*.

"Hi, Mr. Bell!" I climb in and put on my seatbelt. There's room for another four of me back here! Asher turns around and gives me a thumbs-up as hello.

49

"How's the saxophone going?" Mr. Bell asks, smiling over his shoulder at me as he pulls away from the curb.

"Pretty good. We're learning a song called 'Take Five' which is extra fun to play because it's in a totally different rhythm. It's got five beats to a measure instead of four."

"That's Dave Brubeck. I love that song!" He starts counting out the beats. "One, two, three, four, five, one, two, three, four, five," and then whistles the tune. The melody is super hard; we have to play it about half as fast as it's supposed to go. Mr. Bell has it down, though. I've never heard anyone whistle as well as he does.

Asher looks embarrassed. "Dad," he calls out, breaking the word into two syllables.

"No, it's awesome!" I say. "Don't stop!" Asher rolls his eyes at me. His dad goes on a little while longer before giving in to his pouty face. He turns on the radio and drives the rest of the way in silence as Asher and I do dance moves in our seats.

Valentina and her mom are already there when we arrive, and she runs up to us as soon as we walk in. She's wearing her team colors, white and gold, and her long, black curls are tied up in a bun on top of her head. "Hey, Lu! Hi, Mr. Bell!" She takes Asher by the arm, and the two of them run off to go warm up. I follow Mr. Bell to over to the stands where Valentina's mom is sitting.

"Hi, Ms. Perez!" She smiles at me and says hello to Mr. Bell first, kissing him on the cheek.

"Hello, Lu! Thank you so much for coming. Valentina is very happy that you're here. Not too many of her friends have an interest in coming to see her compete." She takes my hand and looks at me with gratitude, her eyebrows raised over little round glasses that make her eyes look huge.

"I do!" I say. "I'm totally into it. I love watching people do things I don't think I could ever do."

"Oh, but you could do it if you practiced!" she insists, looking very serious. "You can be anyone you want to be, if you just see it through." I'm certain she's right, but it's not about that. It's the leotard and all the other girl stuff.

"I know," I say, wanting to change the subject. "Maybe one day." That's what Mom always says to me. It's pretty handy.

Mr. Bell sits next to Ms. Perez, and I sit next to him. They start talking about grown-up things, so I put on my headphones and check my notifications. Ben's at mini-golf with his cousins, and Maddie's posted a video loop of her dad making funny faces. Valentina's been tagged in a photo, so I click on it and see that it's from the trip she took last summer to visit her aunt in Florida. Aunt Mona and her partner, Karen, are standing on either side of Valentina with their hands on her shoulders, smiling big and squinting into the sun. They're at Gay Pride, and Valentina's holding up a sign that says "I Love My Gay Aunts."

Aunt Mona looks like a cool person. She has flowers tattooed all up and down her entire left arm and she's wearing a t-shirt that says "NORMAL" on it, only it's spelled out in rainbow letters like the pride flag. She looks a lot like Valentina, with her dark eyes and curly black hair. I click on her name and scroll through her page. She's got a bunch of different links to videos about things she thinks are important, like teaching little girls to be strong and independent, respecting Native American lands, and making sure that gay people have all the same rights as everyone else. One video catches my eye, though, because it's about a little boy. He's totally adorable, and he looks so happy standing there in the photo with his mom and dad. He's a lot younger than me and the headline says, "Parents Share Story of their Transgender Child."

My heart starts thudding in my chest. I've seen this word before and I know what it means. A transgender person is somebody whose body doesn't match their brain, like a man who feels he's really a woman, or a woman who feels she's really a man. I never thought kids could be transgender, though. That must be me! It makes total sense! I'm in a girl's body, but I want to grow up to be a big, strong, man with a heart of gold

who smells like aftershave and takes care of his family.
Like Dad.

I hit "play." The video starts with photos of a very
pretty but unhappy little girl. She's only two or three
years old, and she looks sad in every picture. Her
mother is telling the story and her voice is filled with
sorrow. She's saying that her daughter, Emma, was a
happy, healthy baby who used to smile a lot. When she
started to talk, though, she kept saying she was a boy.
Emma's mom thought that maybe her daughter was
just confused, or that she would grow out of it, but she
never did. Emma just got more and more determined.
"I'm a boy!" she'd cry, and stamp her little foot. She'd
get sad and quiet whenever she had to dress up in girl
clothes, and she didn't make any friends because she
didn't know who to be. She began to hate herself.

Emma's mom starts to cry, and I realize I'm
holding my breath. She says she loves her child more
than anything else in the world, and the last thing she
would ever want is for her baby to hate herself. She
says it's more important that Emma is happy than that

she be a girl. She says she loves her no matter who she is. Then the gloomy music changes and starts to get more cheerful, because Emma's mom and dad have decided that she can be a boy! Now the pictures show the smile on Emma's face getting wider and wider. They cut her hair short and start calling her "him," and they change his name to Aiden. There are pictures of him swimming in a boy's bathing suit and dancing with a little girl at a party. He's six years old and looks totally like a boy, and he's adorable in his baseball uniform and his little suit with his shining, happy face. His parents love him so much that they not only accept him as their son, they're *proud* of him.

I pull the hood of my sweatshirt over my face so no one will see me crying. I want what Aiden has more than anything in the world.

9

Mom messages me to say that she and Dad are going out to lunch with friends and won't be home when I get back. She tells me to let myself in and eat the lunch she made for me, which is sitting on a plate in the refrigerator. I'm sure it's a salad, so I'm relieved when Asher's dad takes us for a slice of pizza on the way home.

Mr. Bell knows I've been crying, but Asher hasn't noticed. He's too excited from his 2nd place finish in the floor exercise to talk about anything else. It's okay; he did a fantastic job, and I know how hard he worked for that medal around his neck. I tell him how great he was and let him talk as much as he wants to about it.

56

After we eat, he excuses himself to go to the restroom, and Mr. Bell looks at me, full of concern. His pale blue eyes are just like Asher's.

"Are you okay, Lu?"

"Yes," I lie, looking down at the table.

"Really?" I can see that he's worried about me. I wish I could talk to him, but I feel like I need to talk to my own dad first. At least it'll be easier than talking to Mom. She's the one who's always bringing home *blouses* instead of shirts for me, with flowers and bows on them like I'm some kind of gift for someone. She knows I don't like them, but she either keeps forgetting or hoping I'll change my mind.

"Yes," I repeat softly.

"Lu?" he asks, and I look up at him. "You know you can talk to me anytime, right? I mean, if something's going on at home or you just need another grown-up, okay?"

"It's okay, Mr. Bell. Everything's fine at home."

"Well, I just want you to know that I'm here for you if you need me."

"Thanks. That's really nice of you, but I'm okay. Really."

"Asher thinks the world of you, Lu. You're a good friend to him. I know he doesn't have a lot of friends." Mr. Bell looks sad about it, but also like he's used to it.

"Neither one of us has a lot of friends, but the ones we have are really good."

"That's the best way to do it," he says, and Asher returns.

They drop me off at my house and wait for me to get inside the door before driving away. I check the refrigerator and just as I expected, there's a salad sitting there in plastic wrap. I pour myself a glass of grape juice and go up to my room. I'm still thinking about Aiden and his parents, and how happy he looked. I wish I could go back in time and have Mom and Dad do that for *me*, but I keep hearing Mom saying, over and over again in my head, "You're a girl and it's not going to change, so you'd better get used to it." The words are a pain in my chest and a pressure behind my eyes, like my body wants to cry and stop breathing at the same time.

I look at my phone and see I've got plenty of time before they get home. I take off everything but my socks and underpants and go into their bedroom; I'm on tiptoe even though no one else is in the house. I go straight to Dad's dresser and open the drawer where I know his undershirts are, pulling out the one right on top so it will be easier to put back without messing up the rest. It still smells like him, even though it's clean. I slip it over my head and the cotton feels cool against my skin, like a soft shield between me and the world. From his closet, I choose a crisp blue shirt and a pink tie with tiny purple polka-dots. I love my Dad's ties. They're all sorts of colors and patterns and pictures, not just stripes but diamonds and paisleys and tiny little airplanes and sailboats.

In front of the mirror, I button the shirt to the top and pull the collar up so I can do the tie. I put it around my neck with the wide end hanging lower so I have room to make the knot with it. I cross the wide side over the narrow one and bring it around and under twice, but the second time, I bring it up through the neck hole and pull it down inside the second loop. It's easy once you get the hang of it. I tighten the knot and pull it closer to my neck, admiring the way it looks against the shirt.

I go back to the closet and take out the suit Dad wore yesterday since it's already hanging a little sloppy on the hanger. It'll be easy to put back later. His brown wingtip shoes are by the bed, so I pull on the pants and step into them. The pants are falling off me, so I go back to his ties and get one he never wears to use as a belt. In front of the mirror again, I slip on his jacket and hold it shut in front of me. I feel handsome and strong and powerful. I want to be his son and grow into these clothes.

10

It's midnight, and I can't sleep. Mom and Dad turned out the lights and went to bed ages ago, but I'm still tossing and turning. I can't stop seeing Aiden in my mind, whether I close my eyes or not. I can't stop hoping that my parents might love me as much as his parents love him. I can't stop thinking that it's actually possible for me to be a boy!

I'm afraid, though. What if my parents won't let me do it? What if they say it's wrong? That Aiden and his parents are wrong? And what about the kids at school? Would they ever accept me as a boy? They'd probably bully me worse than Asher. Maybe even worse than Cameron. A light bulb goes on in my head: I'm starting middle school next year. Maybe I could go to a different school? One where they didn't already know me as a girl? I could start all over. I could be myself!

It's all way too exciting for me to fall asleep. I close my eyes tightly and switch on the lamp. Once I can open them, I grab my laptop from my desk and bring it into bed with me. Propping my pillows against the headboard, I get under the covers and switch it on. When it finally powers up, I do a search for "transgender kids" and get maybe a zillion links to stories and pictures about kids whose parents have let them be who they are inside. I start a folder with links to articles by teachers, doctors, parents, and the kids themselves so I can send them to my parents. I know I'm going to need it when I tell them.

I'm not sure how they'll take it. Dad says Mom wanted a daughter so badly, when she found out I was coming she cried for days. It's complicated. Mom had a baby sister she loved very much, but she died when they were kids. She named me after her. I know she understands that I'm not the same person, but sometimes I feel like she wishes I were.

Dad's a different story. I get the feeling he doesn't care whether I'm a boy or a girl; he's going to treat me the same way no matter what. He already includes me in pretty much everything he can, so it's not like things would be different between us if I were his son. I'd just be happier being myself.

It's not just about the clothes. It's hard to explain. It's like, as soon as I knew there was a difference between boys and girls, I knew I was a boy. But then Mom told me I wasn't, and so there was that. It didn't matter much until I started school, and then suddenly there was a whole world of people coming at me, saying that I should "act like a girl" and like girly things when all I can do is look over at the boys and feel like I should be there, playing by those rules. There's a certain way to talk and a certain way to walk, and I can't help it; I always do it the boy's way. Even grown-ups call me "young man" sometimes. It's just who I am.

I think I'm a good person. I'm a loyal friend, and I try to do what my parents tell me. I like myself. The problem is, I hate my body. It's wrong on me. I don't know why, and it doesn't matter. One day, I'll grow breasts and then I'll hate it even more. I'd do anything to make it stop, to turn it all around and go back to being born again and come out as a boy. Mom might be disappointed, but at least I'd be happy.

I turn off my computer and return it to my desk. Crawling back under the covers, I switch off the light and close my eyes to try to fall asleep. I inhale deeply and exhale slowly, over and over again until my muscles relax and I begin to feel like I'm sinking into my bed. My mind drifts down the dark, narrow well that leads to my deepest secret and pushes it up like warm water washing over me. I see my body, naked, with my penis where it should be. I don't believe in magic but maybe, if I hold it in my heart strongly enough, it'll be there when I wake up.

11

I'm in the movie theater with Ben, and Maddie keeps texting me. It's okay because the movie is awful. It's rated PG-13, and even though my dad had to buy us the tickets, it's not scary at all. Maggie is saying she wishes we were hanging out this weekend like we do every other, and she's sorry she's so busy with her family. I tell her not to worry, I'll see her tomorrow.

Ben and I are sharing a jumbo tub of popcorn with extra butter and a giant chocolate bar, but we've each got our own drinks. He's rolling his eyes at all the bloody scenes and saying how they do it so much better on TV, where they actually show you the guts. It's true. I can watch way more violent stuff any time I want to at home, but Dad had to be here for this. He's not into horror movies, though, so he walked us in and then left. I'm supposed to message him when we're ready to be picked up.

When the movie ends, we decide to walk through the mall. Ben has some birthday money to spend, and he's looking for sneakers, so we go into a store. While he's trying them on, I walk over to the racks of clothes. They're separated, like always, into men and women, boys and girls. Why is this always so hard for me? Why do I feel like a weirdo every time? Who decided that girls are supposed to want to wear that stuff? You'd have to tie me down to get it on me, and I'd fight you all the way.

I head for the boys' section. When I'm with Mom, she keeps herding me back to the girls' section, but on my own, I sometimes check it out. These clothes make sense to me. They're made for doing things, not looking pretty. They have lots of pockets for holding stuff, and you can crawl around on the ground without ruining them. If a bully is chasing you, you can run away fast. Or maybe fight back. I mean, I've seen girls in dresses fight pretty well, but it always ruins the outfit.

I move through the racks to the boys' shirts. Most of them are boring or ugly, and lots of them have giant brand names splashed across them. My dad always says, "I'm not going to pay my own good money to sell their stinking product," so I walk past them to the button-down shirts. I run my hands through them to feel the fabric, and I get a chill up my spine. It's the boy inside me saying, "Yes!" but the rest of me is worrying about what Mom would say if I brought one home. I'm feeling the sleeve of a green checked shirt when Ben walks up with a shoebox in his hand.

"Hey," he says, a little annoyed, "I was looking all over for you." He's a few inches taller than me, and his shaggy brown hair is plastered to his face with sweat. He's wearing the same team shirt that he wears every day during baseball season, for luck. I once asked him what he does when it gets dirty, and he said, "No problem. I've got four of them." I bet it makes getting dressed in the morning easy.

"Sorry! I was just . . ." I let my voice trail off.

Ben comes up beside me and touches the shirt I'm looking at. "Cool shirt!" he says. "I like the stitching."

"Yeah, I like it a lot." I drop the sleeve and start to walk away.

"Where are you going?" he asks. "Don't you want it? It's only ten dollars." I look at him, and I'm not sure what he reads in my face, but he shakes his head at me.

"I don't get it," he says. "What's the problem? Are you afraid people will think you're a boy? So what? It's no big deal."

"That's just it," I say, tears spilling out of my eyes. "I *am* a boy!" Ben's mouth falls open but he doesn't say anything. He just stands there watching me cry. I'm waiting for him to laugh at me or walk away or punch me but all he does is sigh and put his hand on my shoulder. "C'mon," he says. He takes the shirt off the rack and leads me to the cashier, where he buys it for himself. "It's a nice shirt," he says, and shrugs at me.

We walk over to the coffee shop, where we buy hot chocolate and cookies. We find a place to sit and sip our drinks for a while. After a few minutes, Ben hands the bag with the shirt in it to me.

"Look," he says, "I bought this for you. It's your shirt. You can take it now, or you can take it later, but it's yours. I'll keep it at my house for you if you want."

I'm totally confused. Why would Ben do that for me? That's like, the nicest thing ever!

"Are you kidding?" I ask, afraid that he's going to turn it into a joke.

"No. I get it. You're a boy."

"What?" I'm totally shocked. I never expected this.

"It's okay, Lu. I'm cool with it."

"Really?" I'm almost afraid to believe he's being serious right now.

"Yeah. You're not the only transgender person I know. My cousin, Kate, used to be a boy. Or at least, she was born looking like a boy. I never saw her like that. To me, she's always been this beautiful woman. She's a lot older than us so, you know, she had a hard time back when she first came out. But she's totally happy now, and she's getting married and everything."

"Is that the wedding you're going to in Chicago?"

"Yeah. She's been with Rob for like, forever. He's a good dude."

"That's amazing! Wow! That's so cool!" I let it sink in that my best guy friend is telling me he knows that I'm a boy and he's completely fine with it. I'm not the only transgender person in his life. Suddenly I don't feel so alone anymore.

"Geez, Ben, I'm just . . ." I try to think of what to say, but all that comes out is "thanks."

"No sweat," he says, and fist bumps me. "I've always thought of you as a guy, anyway."

"Really? Why?"

"It's a lot of things. You just seem like a guy. The way you talk. The way you stand. The way you think about things. The stuff you're into. Your clothes. You always wear, like, the least girly thing you can find. I don't know. It just all sort of adds up." I'm smiling and nodding, so he adds, "I never would have said anything to you about it. I mean, you are who you are."

"Thanks, man. I mean it."

"It's cool, Dude," he says with a grin, and we both know that this time, "Dude" means I'm one of the boys.

12

Maddie and I walk down the street to the ice cream shop after school. She's supposed to buy herself a shake whenever she wants to because she's underweight. I'm not sure why, because she eats a ton. I'd say some people are lucky that way, but I know it's actually a problem for her.

We grab a couple of stools at the counter, and she orders a large chocolate shake. They make it in a blender and pour the extra into a small cup for me. We haven't had a chance to hang out yet, and I want to tell her about Ben and the shirt. I have to tell her about me first, though.

We're talking about the play and all the people who didn't try out for it. I'm wishing I was one of them, since Ms. Baxter's probably going to make me wear something awful for the part I don't want to play. But I won't back out because A, I'm no quitter, and B, it would look weird.

"Well, Asher and Valentina are really busy," I start.

"I know," says Maddie. "And Ben's going to that wedding. And Tyler and Olivia told me they have stage fright."

"Andrew was out sick during try-outs, so Ms. Baxter put him in the chorus. He said it's not worth it."

"And Jake has baseball," says Maddie, then quickly stops talking. I know she has a crush on him like all the other girls, but I can see she regrets bringing him up.

"It's okay. I'm over it."

"Really?" She seems happy that I said it.

"Yeah. Whatever," I say, and she breathes a sigh of relief.

"That's great! That's really great."

"I just don't understand why he did it, though. I mean, he's never paid any attention to me before. It was kind of out of nowhere."

"Well, he said he would kiss any girl in the class except you, so we all paid him to do it." Maddie looks at me like she's hoping I'll laugh.

"Wait a minute. Everybody chipped in?"

"Yeah."

"Oh." I get quiet and stare at my cup. "Okay." Neither one of us says anything for a long time.

"Lu?" she asks, after what seems like an hour but is probably more like two minutes. I look up from the spot on the table I've been staring at. "I'm sorry. I really am. We all thought it would be funny. But then I saw the look on your face, and I felt terrible. I just, I didn't know what to say."

I know she's telling the truth, and she does feel bad, but I don't care. I'm not letting her off the hook right now. I'm the one who got hurt, and I'm not going to feel sorry for her.

"Right," I say, and get up from the table. "I have to go home now." I walk out and leave her sitting there with the rest of her shake. Some best friend.

I walk home to my house, a solid knot of anger. I want to kick in car doors and punch through windows but I tighten my muscles instead and put all my focus into walking as fast as I can without running. The birds see me coming and scatter as I approach them, like there's a giant ball of energy that surrounds me and reaches them before I do. The light at the corner turns red and I walk into the crosswalk anyway. Cars blare their horns at me, but I ignore them and keep going. I'm not sure I would care if one hit me. Maybe I want it to.

I'm writing poetry in my head because I can't help it. The words fly into my brain and they happen to rhyme.

> *I don't need you or anybody.*
> *I can do this on my own.*
> *If my best friend chips in her money,*
> *then I'm better off alone.*

75

It's a long walk home and I'm powering myself through it, pumping my legs like a machine and breathing hard. I don't look at the people I pass, only the street and the cars and the trees. I roll around in awful thoughts.

> *Everyone thinks I'm ugly.*
> *I'll always be a freak.*
> *I'll never have what I want.*
> *I'm miserable every week.*
> *I feel like I'm trapped in a box*
> *and it's getting harder to breathe.*
> *I need the pain to end*
> *before it really gets to me.*

Then I remember Ben, and the shirt, and Mom and Dad, and the people who love me, and my friends. It's easy to forget the good things when I feel so terrible.

I'm calm by the time I get home. Mom's in court tonight, so Dad's in the kitchen making dinner. That means we're having sandwiches. He calls them "ham specials," and he's very picky about how you make them. You have to put the mayo on the lettuce side and the mustard on the ham side, or it's ruined. I agree with him totally. You want the tangy mustard on the meat side and the creamy mayo on the salad side, or it doesn't make any sense in your mouth when you bite into it.

"Hi there, sweetie," he says. "Dinner's almost ready."

"Dad, it's like, four o'clock."

"Is it? Well I'm hungry now. You?" he asks, raising one eyebrow.

"Sure," I say, because that little cup of Maddie's shake is all I've had since lunch, which was mostly lettuce.

We sit down to eat and he asks me the usual questions about school.

"Did you write that paper that you had to? The one on the Westward Expansion?"

"Yeah, but it was such a pain. My computer is so slow, I can't stand it! It takes forever to get online and download what I need from school. When can you fix it for me?"

"I fixed it this afternoon." He smiles. "I was tired of listening to you complain about it."

"Thanks! That's awesome, Dad."

"You just needed some more memory. It cost me a lot less than buying you a new one."

"Cool. I'm glad you could do it."

"So I was thinking," he says, "how about I pick you up after school tomorrow? I've got a free day and we could walk along the shore like we used to." I'm surprised he wants to take me on a school day.

"Sure. That'd be great."

Later that night, Cam messages me. Once in a while, when the mood strikes him, he'll fire off a stanza or two of poetry. He always makes me guess who the author is and even though I'd never heard of any of them at first, I'm starting to know who they are.

> *"The caged bird sings*
> *with a fearful trill*
> *of things unknown*
> *but longed for still*
> *and his tune is heard*

on the distant hill

for the caged bird

sings of freedom."

"That's really beautiful," I message back. "And really sad."

"Do you know who wrote it?" It would be easy to cheat and look it up but that wouldn't be any fun, so I guess instead.

"It sounds like it's about slavery. Or civil rights."

"Yes! So which poets wrote about that?"

"Langston Hughes?"

"Good try, but this one is by Maya Angelou. Langston Hughes was earlier."

"I like that it's easy to understand."

"Yes. But it's also very deep. It's not just about civil rights. Even I can relate to it."

"Me, too," I agree after re-reading it, because I can feel the cage around me.

13

"Please don't be mad at me! I'm really, really sorry!" Maddie is messaging me. I silence my phone and set it face down on my desk. I'm not sure how to feel. I get it that Maddie was just going along with everyone else, thinking it would be funny if the cutest boy in class kissed the only girl he said he wouldn't. I know she didn't mean to hurt me, but she did. They all did. Everyone was in on it. I guess I have to let it go, or I won't have *any* friends. I mean, even Ben was in on it. Maybe I shouldn't be so hard on Maddie. I'm just so angry at her!

Boys are different, though. You expect them to make fun of each other. They do it to be funny, and no one's supposed to take it seriously. There's a fine line between goofing on each other and bullying, though, and you can't always tell which is which. Girls are easier to read. They're either nice to you or mean to you, so you always know where you stand. I thought I knew Maddie. I thought I could count on her.

I pull the script for the play out of my backpack. I've been through it so many times that it's getting gray with fingerprints and curled at the edges. I know all my lines by heart, but I keep going over them just to be sure. Every time I get to the protest scene from the '60s, I feel anxious and weird, and I have to stop for a minute. I can do the voice, but I can't be the character. I can't even *think* about being that person. I have to block the picture from my mind so I can finish.

I'm trying to do it now, but my mind is wandering. What am I going to have to wear? Is Ms. Baxter going to put me in a dress? I don't think I could stand that. It's bad enough being in one, but being on stage in one? It'd be like being naked in front of everybody. Her family owns a costume shop, which means we always have amazing costumes for our plays. Who knows what she'll show up with? Probably something that was in style at the time.

I go to my laptop and search for "1960s fashion." I see nothing but dresses, all the way down the page. Women wear pants now; I wonder when that started? I change my search to "When did women start wearing pants?" and learn that there are still certain jobs where I'd have to wear a skirt if I got hired. It's up to the company to decide what their dress code is. In California, though, they made a law that gives women the right to wear pants at work, so if I can't be a boy on the outside, then I'm definitely going to live there.

I'm thinking about women's rights and I realize that the scene in the play is about people who are protesting not just for civil rights, but also against the war in Vietnam. All the kids were against it because there was a draft, and the guys didn't have a choice. If their number got called, then they had to go fight. An awful lot of them were killed. I know that Grandma Sarah used to go to protests, and I've heard Mom talk about her being "an old Vietnam-era hippy." I've *never* seen Grandma in anything but pants.

Excited, I run down the stairs. Mom got home late and she's still working at the kitchen table, answering email.

"Mom? Do we have any old pictures of Grandma Sarah? Like, from the '60s?"

"I think so. They'd be in those big, black binders in the den. Why?"

"For the play. I was looking at costumes online and I thought it would be neat to see how she looked then." It's a little white lie, and I've told so many of them by now that I don't even realize when I'm doing it.

"Why don't you bring them in here and we'll look at them together?"

I run into the den and straight to the bookcase against the far wall. I've never understood why it's in here because no one ever looks at any of the books. They're all dusty and some of them smell like Great-Grandma's basement, musty and green. I pull three giant binders off the bottom shelf and carry them back to the kitchen. It's a lot to manage in one trip, but I'm too excited to make two. I drop the binders on the table with a thud and open the one on top.

"Wait," says Mom, "let's do it in order." She looks at one page from each book and sets them out in front of us from left to right. The first book, she says, is Dad's side of the family. "Are you interested?"

"Yes!"

The photos in the book are so old that almost all of them are black and white. The ones that are even older are a kind of brown that Mom says is called "sepia." Some of them are damaged so badly that you can't make out the faces, but others are as clear as if they were taken yesterday. They're all from a long time ago, and the people are dressed in clothes I've never seen before. The boys are wearing long shorts that gather below the knee, and all the babies are in gowns, no matter whether they're boys or girls. The oldest pictures are studio shots with people posed in and around fancy chairs, but the later ones are snapshots of people on vacation and celebrating holidays. Everyone looks much happier in the later ones.

"Dan," Mom calls out, "do you want to come in here? We're looking at these old pictures of your family."

Dad comes into the kitchen saying, "I don't know who a lot of those people are."

"Really?" I ask, surprised that he keeps photos of strangers. "Why do you still have them?"

"Well, they're all relatives. That's the family history in there, but I only know part of it."

"Who's this?" I point to the oldest picture. It's not even printed on regular paper; it's thicker and more like cardboard. A woman is sitting stiffly in a high-backed chair wearing a dark, long-sleeved dress with buttons all the way up her neck. Her blonde hair is piled up on top of her head and her only jewelry is her wedding ring. She looks stern and resolved, like she's ready for whatever unpleasant thing awaits her.

"I think that's Grandma Robyn's great-grandmother, Anna." He thought for a minute. "She'd be your great-great-great grandmother."

"Yeah, but do you think she was a great grandmother?" I laugh, and he frowns at me before he laughs, too.

"Probably. Although it couldn't have been easy."

"Why?"

"She brought everyone over from the 'Old Country' around the turn of the last century."

"Dan," says Mom, "English, please. Lu doesn't know what the 'Old Country' is."

"It's how we refer to the place the family lived before coming to America. On my side, it's Russia and Ukraine. Your Mom's family is from Russia and Poland."

"Then why don't we speak any of those languages?"

"It was a long time ago," says Mom. "They moved here almost a hundred years ago. All of the kids learned English."

"I don't think my family ever spoke Ukrainian or Russian, though. Yours didn't, either, right, Nicole?" Dad looks at Mom for agreement.

"They spoke Yiddish," she says. "They kept to themselves in the *shtetl*. They only dealt with other Jews."

"No one else wanted anything to do with them," says Dad. "They were never Russians, or Poles, or Ukrainians; they were Jews."

"What's a *shtetl*?" I ask. "Did I say it right?"

"Yes, that was perfect. The Jews were forced to live in towns called *shtetls*. They were segregated off from everyone else, and they were very poor."

"All of your great-great-great grandparents came to America around the year 1900," says Mom. "They left their homes because their lives were in danger. First the Russians went after them, then the Germans. The Jews are the great scapegoats of European history. People are dying of the plague? It must be the Jews! Children are missing? It must be the Jews!" She says this with humor, but it's not funny.

"Why?" I ask. "Why did everyone hate us?"

"Back then," explains Dad, "Jewish people stood out. We all looked a certain way, we all dressed a certain way, and we only married each other. Most people kept a kosher home and followed all the rules about it. There's a lot more to it than not mixing meat and dairy. You have to have separate sets of dishes, and separate forks and knives, and all of that. So you can't ever eat in a restaurant that isn't run by Jews. You stay inside your own circle, and it sets you apart. When there's a whole group of people who look different and act different, it's easy to blame whatever goes wrong on them. Our families left all those things behind in the 'Old Country,' though. Once they got to America, they were more interested in being safe and fitting in."

"They used to accuse the Jews of having all the money," says Mom. "That's still a stereotype here, the 'rich Jew.' But I'll tell you something: You've never seen poorer people than your great-great-great grandparents. They came here to escape the persecution in Europe with nothing but the clothes on their backs. They worked hard and saved every penny, and they managed to build a future for us. It's because of them that we have this wonderful life. We have the right to be exactly who we are because they were brave enough to risk everything and come to America. We need to be grateful for that." Her words echo in my mind. *We have the right to be exactly who we are.*

"That's right," says Dad. "Your great-great grandfather came here from Ukraine all by himself when he was sixteen years old. His father had come before him and set up a pushcart, which was literally a cart full of whatever you were selling that you pushed down the street. They were peddlers. I think they sold kitchen tools and sharpened knives. They walked all day, from sunrise to sundown, hoping they'd make enough money to be able to buy something to eat." I think of the people who go from person to person on the boardwalk, holding out arms full of jewelry or keychains or t-shirts. Next time I'm there, I'll buy something.

89

14

Back at my desk, I'm holding a photo of Grandma Sarah that we found in the last of the three binders. It's 1967, and she's about twenty, sitting with her friends on a blanket in the park. She's wearing a solid-colored blouse with long, poofy sleeves that are gathered at the wrist, and an open vest with a busy print on it. A narrow paisley headband keeps her long, blonde hair from falling across her face. The most important thing to me, though, is her faded, wide-legged jeans with the giant peace-sign patches on them. It's an outfit I could handle wearing on stage; in my head, it's just pants and a shirt. I take a picture of the photo with my phone so I can keep it with me and tuck the original into a corner of the frame that holds my honor roll award.

I've got three messages from Maddie, one from Asher, and one from Michael. I'm still mad at Maddie, and Asher can wait, but Michael wants to talk about our classroom debate tomorrow, so I message him back first. We're on the side that's against allowing girls to play football with boys. No one in the class wanted to do it, so Mrs. Rubin wrote everyone's name on a small slip of paper, put them into a bowl, and pulled out two team captains. When Michael got picked, he chose me first.

"I can't believe I have to do this," says Michael. "The girls are going to hate me."

"It depends on what you say. We need a plan!"

"How about if we have three main points and we all just stick to them? We can come up with them now and tell the team tomorrow."

"Cool. Any ideas?"

"We could say the boys would be afraid of hurting the girls so they wouldn't play as hard. It wouldn't be the same."

"That's brilliant! I love it!" I'm happy because it doesn't make anyone look bad. The guys are just trying to be nice. Way to go, Michael! "Okay, so sort of on the same topic, it wouldn't be very gentlemanly to tackle a girl. Boys aren't supposed to hit girls. They're supposed to be nice to them."

"Good one! Yes!"

There's a long pause while both of us are trying to think of a third point. Finally, it comes to me. "Some of the boys are a lot bigger than the girls. It's an unfair advantage."

"The girls could get hurt really badly," adds Michael.

"The same is true for some of the boys," I say, feeling like I have to defend myself for some reason.

"Okay, but that's not the side you're on! Stick to the plan!"

"Right. I will."

"Cool! I think we're good. See you tomorrow!"

I look at Maddie's messages. The first one says, "Hello?" The second says, "Hello-oo? Are you there?" The last one says, "Message me when you can." I figure it's okay if I don't write back. Maybe I'm busy?

Asher's message is a link to a music video; we're always sending each other stuff like that. It's the new song from Losers and Lemons, and he knows I'm not into them, but his message says, "You HAVE to see this!!!" so I click "play." The music begins and it's just okay, but I can tell right away that the video is going to be cool. It starts in outer space and the camera zooms in fast, past stars and planets all the way through the solar system to the Earth and down through clouds until a city comes into view and gets closer and closer until you can see the buildings and then just one skyscraper and one man on its roof, standing on the ledge and teetering thousands of feet above the street, looking like he's going to jump off. When he does, I gasp, but instead of falling he floats up into the air, his t-shirt flapping in the wind. Then he begins to fly through the city.

He sees a landlord throwing a woman and her two kids out of their apartment because they haven't paid the rent, but as he floats past, the scene changes and the landlord is giving them bags of groceries. Through the window of a school, he sees a group of bullies about to pounce on a boy in a dance studio, dressed in tights. He passes by and now the all of boys are dancing. There's a squad of police officers with shields and batons and a crowd of rioters headed for each other; as he flies overhead, the police line up to protect a peaceful march instead. He sees a woman walking into a restroom but an angry man stops her and points her in the other direction. I realize she's transgender, mostly because she's tall and her shoulders are broad. She's beautiful, but the look on her face is tragic, like the man has just told her she's garbage. The hero flies by, and now the man and the woman are friends, laughing together and talking. They say goodbye as she walks happily into the ladies' room. He sees a man with a gun, about to rob another man, but once his shadow crosses them, they're both coaxing a kitten out from under a parked car. Suddenly he's back at the beginning, standing on the ledge of the skyscraper looking impossibly sad and ready to jump. Just when you think he's going to do it, someone takes his hand. He turns around, and it's the transgender woman, looking up at him in a way that says, "You are loved. Don't jump." Behind her are all the people from the video, everyone the hero touched, reaching out to him. He steps down off the ledge, and they pull him into the crowd as the music fades out. By the time it's over, my tears have totally blinded me. I can hardly see the screen.

"You're right," I message Asher. "That was amazing."

15

Maddie finds me in the schoolyard during recess. "Why aren't you talking to me? I can't stand it anymore!"

"I'm not 'not talking' to you," I tell her. Even though I'm sort of not.

"You didn't answer any of my messages last night."

"I was busy. I've got a lot of stuff to do with the debate and the band, and the play and everything."

"Me too," she says, hurt.

"Well," I start, changing the subject, "Michael and I talked last night, and we came up with some good stuff for our side. It wasn't easy. You're lucky you get to be on the good side."

"Yeah. To be honest, though, I don't know if girls should play football."

"Seriously?" I'm shocked. I thought Maddie the jock would be all over it.

"Yeah. I mean, we're better than that, aren't we? Do we really need to throw each other on the ground to score goals? It seems so, I don't know. . ." she searches for the word, "barbaric."

"Geez, that's a good point, Mads. I wish we'd thought of it."

"You can use it if you want to."

"Thanks."

"Can you believe what happened this morning?"

"With the snake?"

"Yes!" she says, plainly horrified. "They shouldn't allow that at school."

"You mean the whole 'eating the mouse' thing?"

"Yes! Please! That was awful. Erik never should have brought it to school in the first place."

"But it's beautiful! That snake was amazing."

"So was the mouse!"

"Animals eat animals," I say with a shrug. "It's nature."

"Okay, but I don't want to see it! I need to go rescue some mice from the pet store now."

"Your mom would never let you in the house with them."

"True. Anyway, you want to go get a shake with me after school?"

"I can't. My dad's picking me up. He's got the day off so we're going to the shore." I'm glad I already have an excuse because even though we're standing here talking to each other, I'm not finished being angry with her. Maybe I'm just disappointed. She used to be my sidekick, but now I feel alone.

* * *

The debate goes well and Mrs. Rubin congratulates our team on finding good ways to argue our points without being insulting to girls. Michael looks relieved and proud. The other side wins anyway, which we all knew was going to happen. At least it was fun, and it took up enough time for us to skip math for the day. Dad picks me up, and we drive across the bridge into town. We head for the beach and park the car, then race each other down to the sand.

Dad and I walk the shore in silence. Sometimes his hand holds mine, sometimes it's on my shoulder. I look mostly at my feet and his, examining his toes inside his flip flops and imagining my feet that big. We usually don't talk much when we do this. It's more about just being together, smelling the air and feeling the breeze. We watch the sea gulls bicker over fish scraps and tiny crabs furiously dig their way deeper into the sand. It's windy but warm, and the sun feels sweet on my face. Dad's pale pink shirt flaps noisily behind him as we walk. A long time passes before he sighs deeply.

"There's something I want to talk to you about, Lu." Oh, no! I hope my parents aren't getting divorced!

"Okay," I say, swallowing hard and preparing myself for the worst.

"I want you to know that your mother and I love you very much." Here it comes. This sounds exactly like the beginning of "The Divorce Speech" that Ben told me about. He's getting ready to tell me he's leaving us.

"I never want to hurt you," he continues, "or make you feel like you can't talk to me. I want you to know that I love you no matter what." He looks at me like he's waiting for me to say something, so I nod to let him know I'm listening but I'm just holding my breath and waiting for him to drop the "D" bomb.

"Lu," he says, "I'm sorry. I didn't mean to do it. It was an accident. I feel terrible about it. I never would have gone looking for it, but it was right there." I have no idea what he's talking about. I try to think if there's anything I hid in my room and forgot about, but there's nothing.

"I turned on your computer and I saw it. It was right there."

The fog in my brain gives way to a light so harsh that I feel like my head is going to explode. WHAT

DID HE SEE? WHAT DOES HE KNOW? WHAT'S GOING TO HAPPEN TO ME? OH, NO! OH, NO! OH, NO! OH, NO! OH, NO! OH, NO!

"Lu!" Dad has dropped to his knees in front of me with his hands on both of my arms. "Calm down, honey. It's all right." I'm shaking so hard that my teeth are chattering even though I'm probably getting sunburned right now. "Here," he says, "sit down," and pulls me into the sand beside him. He puts his arm around me tightly and whispers in my ear.

"I love you. It's okay. You're fine."

"What did you see?" I ask, so softly that I'm surprised he can hear me.

"When I fixed your laptop, I had to download a program. You had left a website open, about transgender kids. I couldn't help myself after that. I looked and saw you had a folder full of links. I'm sorry."

I can't speak. There's nothing to say. He already knows everything.

"Lu," he says evenly, "do you think you're a boy?"

"Yes." My voice is even softer than before.

"Are you sure?"

"Yes," I say with more confidence. I look up into his kind brown eyes. I notice his hair is getting gray around his temples and I think about my own, which feels so wrong on me. "I know I'm a boy. I always have."

"I see." He takes a deep breath. "That settles it, then. We'll have to work this out." He sounds so definite that it scares me a little.

"What do you mean?"

"Don't you worry about that. Let me take care of it."

"Are you going to send me away and make me be a girl?" I imagine there are training camps for girls sort of like military schools for boys, where they force you to walk like a lady and put on make-up.

"What?" Dad practically shouts it. "Don't be ridiculous, Lu! We'd never send you away." He pulls me closer and hugs me so tightly that all I can smell is his aftershave.

"What does 'Let me take care of it' mean, then?"

"It means that this is a problem for your parents to solve, not you. You just be who you are."

"Really?"

"Really."

"What if I want to be your son?"

"Then you'll be my son. You can be my rhinoceros if you want to, as long as you're my kid."

I put it on the shirt that Ben bought for me and admire my reflection in the mirror. After I told him about it, Dad insisted we pick it up on the way home from the beach. With the green checked cotton tucked neatly inside my jeans, I can almost see the boy inside me. For a minute, I consider grabbing the scissors from my desk and cutting off all of my hair, but I decide not to. The shirt is enough for now.

Dad knocks on my door. I tell him to come in.

"I thought you might be needing this," he says, handing me one of his belts. "I cut it down to fit you. Let's see if I got it right." He kneels and helps me thread it through the loops of my jeans. They're girls' jeans, but I don't think anyone would notice. "Yep," he says, satisfied. "Perfect. Never wear a shirt tucked in without a belt. It's funny looking."

We both go downstairs to the kitchen where Mom is already halfway out the door on her way to work. She looks at my outfit and raises one eyebrow. "Is that for the play?"

"Nicole!" says Dad, and I can tell he's warning her to be quiet about it.

"What did I say?" she shrugs.

"Nothing. We'll talk about it later," he says, eyeing me.

"All right then. You two have a good day. I love you both!"

Mom leaves and Dad drops me off at school. "You have fun, now," he says. "Just be yourself and we'll deal with whatever comes up. I'm going to have a talk with your mom as soon as I can. Don't move too fast, okay? One step at a time."

Lucas Hasten

I get out of the car like a brand-new person. I don't ever remember feeling this happy. It's way better than getting a birthday present or going to a concert or anything else that I can think of. I'm going to be my dad's son! I feel ten feet tall as I step into the schoolyard, but the minute I see Sam and Noah, everything changes. Suddenly I'm scared they're going to notice my shirt and make a big deal out of it. I wish I'd thought to wear something else underneath so I could take it off if I needed to. Oh, well, too late for that. I make my way over to Valentina, Michael, and Ben.

"Nice shirt," says Ben with smile.

"Thanks. I almost bought it for you but I figured it'd look better on me!" I laugh and Ben gives me a soft punch in the arm.

"Yeah? Well I'm an extra-large. Remember that for next time."

"It looks awesome on you, Lu," says Valentina. "You should get more like that!"

"Thanks! Maybe I will."

106

When Maddie arrives, she says she likes my shirt so much that she wants one for herself. Ben and Michael run off to play ball until the bell rings and Valentina brings up last night's episode of *Tattoo Mistakes*. We're laughing about a guy whose tattoo said something in Japanese script that turned out to mean "stupid eggplant" – which is a terrible insult in Japan – when we hear Asher screaming.

Across the schoolyard, Sam and Noah are pushing Asher to the ground as a small crowd gathers around them. We run right over, but what can we do? They've got him on the grass, and they're rolling him onto his stomach as they pin his arms behind his back. He's yelling, "Quit it! Quit it!" and he's fighting back hard, but he doesn't stand a chance against two guys who are both bigger than he is. I'm looking around wildly for a grown-up, but of course there aren't any here or Sam and Noah wouldn't doing this right now. Ben and Michael are all the way on the other side of the building and there's no one to help Asher.

I remember what Mr. Bell said about how Asher thinks the world of me, how I'm such a good friend to him. I think of the video that Asher sent me and the hero who wanted to save everyone but himself. In the end, they all saved him. I realize that I have to help Asher, or I'm not worth anyone helping me. I push through the crowd to Sam and Noah while the other kids stand back, surprised.

"Leave him alone!" I yell.

"What's it your business, He-Man?" sneers Noah.

"Get off him!"

"Get out of here, Miss Piggy," says Sam as he reaches inside the back of Asher's pants to pull them down. Asher is crying and screaming, and his face is so red that I'm afraid he's going to pass out. His nose is bleeding.

"GET OFF HIM!" I scream, and rush straight at Sam, knocking him to the ground. I want to punch him, but I won't because it's not worth getting into any more trouble than I already am. I sit on his chest instead, although most of my weight is resting on my hands, which have his arms pinned to the ground. Noah runs away as Sam struggles against me, cursing. It's the first time I've ever been glad I'm bigger than a boy. He's throwing his fists and kicking his legs, but there's not much he can do in that position. Finally, he runs out of steam and stops. We're surrounded by a wall of kids watching us.

"I'm getting up now," I say. "But I'm going straight to the Head of School and telling him what you just did to Asher."

"Oh yeah?" he says, looking at the crowd, "just wait till I get you alone."

"I'll tell him about that too, now. Let's see, what should I say? 'Sam tried to pull off Asher's pants and said he'd to do the same thing to me as soon as he got me alone.' In front of all these witnesses. Have fun in detention."

17

I'm sitting with the Head of School in his office. Dr. Petersen is shaking his head at me. "I know that you wanted to help Asher, but that was very dangerous, Lu. You could have been hurt. You should have found an adult."

"There was no one around, Dr. P. I tried."

"Still. You shouldn't have gotten involved. I really should give you detention, too, you know. You should have gone to find someone."

"By the time I did that, it would have been too late."

"I understand. I do." He looks down at his desk, helpless for a minute. "We've called Asher's mother to come take him home. Do you want us to call your parents?"

"No," I say, "what for? I'm fine."

"You're sure?"

"Yes."

"All right. At any rate, Sam and Noah will be dealt with. You have nothing to worry about."

"I'm not worried about me," I say. "Asher's the one they beat up on."

"I'm going to do something about that, now that I know." He looks at his watch. "Do you think you're ready to go back to class now?"

"Can I see Asher first, please?"

"Anita will give you a hall pass. He's in the nurse's office."

When I stop by Anita's desk, she gives me a cookie as well as a hall pass. She pats me on the back as she sends me off to see Asher. I've got a cookie for him, too. I walk in and find him sitting on the cot with his

111

head back and tissues jammed up his nose. His t-shirt is ripped but other than that, he looks fine.

"Hi, Asher."

He jumps off the cot and throws his arms around me. "Lu! You saved me! Thank you, thank you, thank you!"

"Come on, it's not that big a deal."

"Yes it is. I was screaming and screaming and no one would help me. It was horrible!"

"I'm sorry that happened to you. I should have done something the last time they started pushing you around." I realize I'm still holding his cookie so I hand it to him.

"It's okay," he says, taking it from me. "Anita?" I nod.

He takes a bite and starts chewing even though the bloody tissues are still hanging out of his nose. "You know," he says once he swallows, "you didn't have to . . . I mean, I didn't expect . . . I mean, you know, it's not . . ." His voice trails off. I think he's trying to say that since I'm a girl, it's not my job help him fight.

"Can I tell you a secret, Asher? A big one?"

"Sure."

"I'm really a boy."

"Well, duh," says Asher.

"What do you mean, 'Well, duh'?"

"Geez, Lu, you think I didn't know that already? It's kind of obvious."

"Really?" That's pretty much what Ben said. *It just all sort of adds up.*

"Um, YEAH." He laughs. "I'm just glad *you* finally figured it out."

I need to pee, and I feel weird about using the girls'
room. If I'm a boy, then I don't belong in there. Or at
least, the girls wouldn't want me in there. I can't go
into the boys' room, though. I don't know what would
happen. I guess I have to keep using the girls' room
until something changes.

I walk inside and into an empty stall. The seat is a
total mess, like the last person squatted over the bowl
without sitting on it and had terrible aim. Gross! I
leave the stall and push open the door of another. At
least this seat only has a few drops on it. I grab a wad
of toilet paper and wipe it clean, then I line the seat

carefully with paper just like Mom showed me when I was little. I undo my belt and drop my pants, holding up the tails of my shirt to make sure they don't fall in the toilet. It would be so much easier if I could just stand!

I hear a couple of girls walk into the restroom. They're talking about a boy they like and giggling about how cute he is.

"His eyes are amazing," says one.

"And he's got the greatest smile!" says the other.

"I know! He totally belongs on TV, he's so gorgeous." I can't help it; I wish they were talking about me.

"I heard he kissed Lu!" I should have known it was Jake Ruggiero they were so busy drooling over.

"Yeah, but it was just a joke. She's a cow. They paid him to do it."

"Did you hear she body-slammed Sam? For real. He was beating up Asher and she charged him."

"Awesome! I'm glad *somebody* did it."

115

I hide in the stall and wait for both of them to leave before I do. I'm surprised by how little I care about the "cow" comment. I'm not a cow. But I'm not a girl, either. I get it. I'm a weirdo. They don't know what to make of me.

I go back to class, and Mrs. Rubin gives us a paper to read and a writing prompt. It's about spiders, which almost everyone hates, and the prompt is, "What is the main idea of this article? Use evidence to support your answer." Even though they're creepy, it turns out that spiders help humans a lot. They eat so many bugs who eat our food that without them, humans might not survive. Mom told me they also eat mosquitoes, so when we find one in the house she traps it under a drinking glass and sets it free outside. Sometimes I see that spider in the glass and think: That's exactly how I feel.

We finish our assignment, and Mrs. Rubin dismisses us for play rehearsal. Maddie, Michael, and I head for the multi-purpose room talking about how almost nobody had their lines memorized last time. A group of boys I hardly know are crowded around the lockers; as we approach them, one points at me.

"Here comes 'Big Louie'!" he says.

"Better watch out!" says another, backing away from us. "She's a bulldozer!"

"Shut up!" growls Michael, and I whisper a thanks.

I walk past them, ignoring them completely. Their words hurt, but they also make me smile inside. They think they're making fun of me because I'm a girl. But if you turn it around in your head and think about me as a boy, then they're are actually giving me a compliment. "Big Louie," huh? I like the sound of it.

"I'm going to the pet store today," says Maddie. "Anybody want to come?"

"I'd go but I'm getting paid to tutor my little brother." Michael makes a cash register "ca-CHING" sound.

"I'll go with you," I say. I know *someone* has to keep her from buying any mice! Maddie's heart is so big, she'll want to take home the whole tank of them. She won't even eat meat anymore because she can't bear the thought of people killing animals. I totally respect that, but for me, I think since humans are at the top of the food chain, it's natural for us to eat them. What's *not* okay is making them suffer.

After school, we walk two blocks up to the avenue and five blocks down to the pet store. There aren't any animals in the window, but once you walk in, there's nothing but tanks and cages as far as you can see. I like to come here to look at the lizards and snakes. Some of them are beautiful, with colors that shine only in certain light, and sometimes the people who work here let me hold them. The hamsters and gerbils are pretty cute, too, and I love to watch them fill up their cheeks with kernels of dried corn. There's a tank in the corner full of tiny white mice and Maddie's face is pressed up against it.

"Maddie, you can't."

"Maybe I can," she says. "I'll think of a way."

"Your mom would never let you keep them. You know that. She'll totally freak out if you even bring them in the house."

"What if I she doesn't know? What if I keep them with me and take them everywhere?"

"How in the world are you going to do that? You're crazy!"

"Here!" she pulls me over to a display holding what look like stuffed animals at first. I realize they're hamster pouches; soft little egg-shaped purses with netting across the top so the hamster can breathe, and a strap for wearing them over your shoulder.

"You're nuts," I say. "Come on, let's go get you a shake." I take her firmly by the arm and lead her out of the store. We walk down to the ice cream shop, and she orders her usual. The woman behind the counter winks as she pours off the extra for me, and we grab a table in the back.

"I really want them, Lu. I'm serious."

"Maddie, your Mom is a crazy cleaning person. She can't handle a speck of dust on the piano. Do you really think she's going to let you keep mice in a cage?"

"No," she admits sadly. "But I still feel like I have to do it. To make up for the one I saw get eaten. I

119

already have him picked out, and a friend for him, too!"

"Maddie, stop. You're just going to be disappointed."

We both get quiet. I know she's thinking up a plan to get her way, but I'm thinking about the talk I had with Dad. I need to tell her about it. She's supposed to be my best friend, and I've already told Ben and Asher.

"I need to tell you something," I start.

"Lu, I KNOW my mom won't let me keep the mice!"

"No, no. Not that. Something else."

"Oh. Okay." Maddie sets her shake aside and folds her hands in front of her on the table, making a point of giving me her full attention.

"So, um. . . I talked to my dad and told him I'm a boy and I always have been, and he actually said okay, and he was going to talk to Mom about it, and Ben knows, and Asher knows, and I wanted to tell you first, but I didn't have a chance and so now you know."

"Now I know what?" She looks confused.

"That I'm a boy."

"But you don't have a . . .well, you know." She casts her eyes downward. "You're a girl 'down there'."

"That's just my body. My brain is a boy."

"Is that possible?" She's surprised, but definitely not upset.

"Well I'm here, aren't I?

She looks at me for a while, thinking. I can tell she's trying to figure out what it means, but I already know she's going to be fine with it.

"Are you sure about this?"

"Yes. Like I said, I talked to my dad about it."

"Um . . . okay. So are you like, going to change or something?" She starts sucking the straw in her shake again.

"I don't know. I don't think so. Not right now anyway. I'm just going to be who I am."

"Do you want me to change? Do I have to do anything different?"

"No! I'm still the same person. You don't have to change anything."

121

"Okay," she says, finishing her shake. "So, can we go back and look at the mice again?"

I'm sound asleep when a door slams. I wake up
with a start and see, through the crack of my bedroom
door, that the lights are on in the hallway. It must be
midnight, and my parents are still up.

"Quiet!" I hear Dad whisper-shout. "You'll wake
him up."

"Him? Seriously? Him? You're calling our
daughter 'him' now?"

"Look, Nicole, I know a lot about this – "

"I don't want to hear it."

"Nicole – "

"You're not a doctor, Dan."

"Fine, then. Let's take him to a doctor."

"Fine!" says Mom, like she's just ended the conversation.

"Honey," says Dad, not willing to leave it there, "please try to stop taking this so personally. It isn't about you. "

"What's that supposed to mean?" Mom fumes. "Are you saying I'm being selfish? I don't think you have any idea what you're talking about Dan, because this is most certainly not about me. This is about my daughter ruining the rest of her life at the tender age of eleven. Eleven, Dan! She's far too young to be making this decision."

"It's not a decision, hon. It's who he is. Who he's always been."

"How do you know that? How does *she* even know that? She has no idea what it means to be a woman. Did you know what it meant to be a man when you were eleven years old?"

"I knew I was a boy, that's for sure. And you knew you were a girl. Well, Lu knows he's a boy."

"Lu doesn't know where she's left her keys half the time! Are you seriously telling me she's got this figured out? You're not doing her a favor by going along with it, either, you know. She needs to give being a woman a chance. Lots of girls go through this."

"Look. We have to take him seriously. We need to make sure he has the tools he's going to need to – "

"I can't do this right now, Dan. It's late and I'm tired, and I've got court in the morning. I'm going to sleep." I hear their bedroom door close and Dad's footsteps on the stairs. A minute later, the muffled sound of the TV creeps upstairs. I guess Dad's not going to bed.

More awake than I want to be, I notice my phone flashing red with a message. I reach for it and see Cam has sent me a snippet of poetry. Tonight is Robert Frost, one of his favorites. In the dark of my room, my phone glows with his words:

> *Two roads diverged in a wood, and I –*
> *I took the one less traveled by,*
> *And that has made all the difference.*

125

Michael and I are rehearsing the 1920s scene. I'm the bartender, and he's the customer.

"What'll it be, Jack?"

"How about a 'Rusty Nail'?" he says. Ms. Baxter told us that's the name of a drink, but I pull out an actual rusty nail and hand it to him.

"Wait, Lu," calls Ms. Baxter. "When you take out the nail, you have to hold it up for everyone to see or they won't get the joke."

"Oh, okay!" I do it again and this time, I pull out the nail and show it to the audience as I say the line.

"Here you go, Buddy." She nods happily so we keep going.

"What about a 'White Russian'?"

"We don't ask people where they're from around here."

"Mai-tai?"

"It's perfectly nice. Goes well with your suit."

"Margarita?"

"You must be thinking of someone else."

It's hard for us to get through the scene without cracking up, but we finish, and Ms. Baxter calls for a break. Her phone buzzes.

"That's it! They're here! Come on, kids!" She leads us out the door and down the front stairs of the school to the driveway where a truck is parked. The driver gets out, and she kisses him on the cheek; he looks like he could be her brother. Together, they open the back of the truck and start unloading boxes onto the curb. "Everybody take one and bring it back to the rehearsal room."

One by one, we get all the boxes inside. There must be twenty, and they're all full of costumes and props. Ms. Baxter has set up rolling racks in the room, and we start unpacking everything to hang up the clothes. I'm trying to keep myself from tearing open every box to search for a pair of jeans like Grandma's, so I work as fast as I can to get through them.

The costumes are fantastic. We've got flapper dresses that hang straight down with fringe at the bottom and pin-striped gangster suits for the 1920s scene; I'm happy to see there's a white shirt with a red vest in there for the bartender. There are army uniforms for the '40s and colorful sweaters with giant shoulder pads for the '80s. I go through box after box, hurriedly hanging up shirts and pants and skirts and dresses before someone finally opens the box with the costumes for the '60s in it. It's full of scarves, hats, and headbands. We take them out, and I'm thrilled to see six pairs of faded, wide-legged jeans underneath. I can't believe how lucky I am! Everything else in there

The Sign Around My Neck

is so over-the-top, especially the girls' clothes. Ms. Baxter comes over and starts going through the box.

"Oh, these are fabulous! They're going to look fantastic on stage." She pulls out dress after dress and to me, they're all the same: Awful. None of them have sleeves, and they're all gathered at the waist to look like an hourglass. Some have polka-dots, and some have flowers, and some even have bows near the chest. I would die if she made me wear one of those. She keeps digging and digging, and it looks like finally she's found the one she's looking for. She holds it up to show me, and it's even worse than the others. You know the sign they put on the door to the ladies' room? The one with the woman who's basically wearing a triangle? That's what it looks like. A great big triangle with the top cut off for your head to go through it! The next thing I know, she's holding that horrible thing up against my back.

"Oh yes," she says, "This will fit you perfectly!"

"But I saw all those jeans in there," I cry, pointing at the box. "Can't I wear those?"

129

"Oh, no! Absolutely not. Those are for the boys who are playing the protesters. I can't have you wearing the same thing as them!"

21

I go straight home after school. Maddie's messaging me to meet her at the pet store again, but I ignore her. Cam's messaging me, too, but I can get back to him later. I feel like I'm going to explode, and I need to talk to Dad, but when I walk in the door, I'm surprised to see that Mom is already home, cleaning the oven. I don't want to look her in the eye because I know how mad she is at Dad and how disappointed she is in me. Could this day get any worse?

"Hi, honey! How was your day?"

"Fine." I open the refrigerator, grab an apple, and head up to my room.

131

"Wait a minute! I got you something. Come back here." I wonder if she's feeling bad about last night. Does she know I heard her? Maybe she's trying to make it up to me. I turn around and go back to the kitchen while Mom's washing the oven goop off her hands. "Hang on a minute, let me go get it."

She leaves and comes back with a shopping bag from the clothing store. Pulling out a blouse, she holds it open, explaining how it's got pockets like I always ask for and sleeves that come down to just above the elbow instead of stopping just below the shoulder. Sure, I think, but it's still got these tiny little daisies on it! You can't see what they are unless you're really close but *I* know they're there. Plus, the collar is rounded. What's up with that?

"And wait! Look at this!" Out of the bag comes the thing I've been dreading most in the world, more than the ugly blouse and the ugly dress. "I got you your first bra!"

I feel myself get up from my chair, but I'm not in control anymore.

"No! No, no, no! There's no way you're putting
that on me! I swear to you, I'll run away forever if you
try to make me wear it! I'll hate you for the rest of my
life!" I run up to my room and slam the door as hard as
I can. Taking the chair from my desk, I push it up
against the door and sit down on it so she can't come
in. I'm breathing so fast and hard that my head is
feeling funny. I close my eyes and imagine myself
somewhere else. On the beach, with Dad. I hear Mom's
footsteps coming closer and her voice pleading, "Lu!
Honey! Let me in! Talk to me! Please!" She's knocking
on the door, but all I can hear is the water, the waves,
and the wind.

A long time passes before I feel like I can form words. Checking my phone, I see that Maddie and Cameron both messaged me again about an hour ago. Cam's been so sad lately; I don't have the energy to deal with him right now.

"I don't know what I'm going to do." It takes Maddie less than a minute to message me back.

"About what?"

"About Ms. Baxter. About my mom. About everything." I'm glad I'm typing because if I was talking, I'd be screaming.

"What happened?"

"Ms. Baxter said I absolutely have to wear a dress for the '60s."

"You NEVER wear dresses!!!"

"I know, right?! Not only that, but it's the UGLIEST DRESS IN THE WHOLE WORLD!" I can't get the picture of it out of my mind now. It's all I see when I close my eyes.

"Really?"

"YES!!! Trust me!"

"Wow. I'm sorry! ☹☹☹ Can you talk to her about it?"

"She already said no."

"Maybe your dad can talk to her?"

"Maybe. If my mom doesn't get in the way. SHE BROUGHT HOME A BRA FOR ME TODAY! I feel like I want to die."

"I'll jump for joy when my mom brings one home for me! LOL"

"LOL. Not me." The LOL is there for her because I don't really feel like laughing.

"I guess that's how you know you're not a girl, huh?"

"It's only one thing. There are lots."

"I thought you said your dad was okay with it?"

"I did. But my mom isn't."

"Oh. That blows. I'm sorry! ❤❤❤"

"Thanks."

"What are you going to do?" I can't think of an answer and a lot of time goes by before she messages me again.

"Do you want to come stay at my house? Mom says it's okay." I'm surprised she talked to her mother.

"Did you tell her about me?"

"Yes. You're not mad at me, are you?"

"No, it's fine. I hope everyone will know soon."

"So do you want to come? My dad says he'll talk to your dad."

"That's really nice of him. Thank him for me. I'm staying here for now, though."

"You sure? We can make popcorn and watch movies!"

"I'm sure. You'll just try to make me spit something out of my nose. LOL"

"You know me too well! LOL"

I say goodbye and open my laptop, my heart still pounding. I start an email to Mom with the subject heading, "This is who I am!" and nothing in the box but the links I saved last week. I find the video about Aiden and include that, too. I'm about to click "send" when I think again and scroll down to the bottom of the list, where I write, "AND DON'T BUY ME ANY MORE BLOUSES!"

I think about messaging Cam, but I'm still too upset to try making him feel better. I know he'd listen to me if I wanted to talk, but it's too much to say by text. I haven't told him I'm a boy yet, and he's almost like my brother. He'll be fine with it, for sure, but I want to do it in person. I pull out my saxophone and start to play instead, and the measured breathing that it forces me to do helps calm me down. I play "Take Five" over and over again until the melody comes smoothly and easily, until my fingers know the notes before my brain does.

Eventually I hear Dad get home from work. It's quiet for a while, then I hear muffled voices growing louder, and I can tell they're arguing. I can just make out Dad telling Mom to calm down when the phone rings. She says "Hello," and then, "I'll be right over!" A few minutes later I hear the front door close and the sound of her car driving away.

Dad comes upstairs and knocks on my door. By now I've moved the chair back to my desk and I'm sitting on my bed. I tell him to come in.

"Hi, Sweetie." He's taken off his tie but he's still dressed for work in a blue suit and a white shirt with tiny blue diamonds on it. He comes over and sits down next to me.

"Hi, Dad."

"I heard you had a rough time with Mom."

"Yeah," I say, and leave it there.

"Don't worry, Lu. She'll move past it. She just has to get there in her own way."

"What am I supposed to do in the meantime?"

"About what?"

I tell him about Ms. Baxter and the dress, and about the bra.

"Well," he says, "I'll talk to your mother about the bra. I'm not sure what I can do about the play, though. The costumes are up to Ms. Baxter."

"I know," I say. "I guess I could back out."

"Do what feels right to you, honey." His words hang in the air for a minute.

"Dad?"

"Yes?"

"When I'm your son, are you going to stop calling me 'Sweetie' and 'Honey'?

"I don't know. I hadn't thought about it." He looks at me, concerned. "Do you want me to stop?"

"I'm not sure. I mean, most dads don't call their sons 'Honey,' do they? That's kind of a girl thing."

"Then I'll stop."

"But that makes me sad."

"Then I won't."

139

"It'll sound weird, though." His furrows his brow and frowns, thinking.

"How about we come up with something special just for you, then?"

"Like what?"

"I don't know yet. Something will click eventually. Let's give it a little time."

"Okay, Dad."

My alarm goes off, so I get up and go to the bathroom. Dad's in there, shaving. He leaves me alone and comes back in when I'm finished.

"Where's Mom?" I ask. Dad looks sad and helpless for a minute.

"She spent the night at Aunt Caroline's house."

"Why? Is she angry?"

"No, she's just keeping her company."

"Is Aunt Caroline okay?"

Dad looks like he's trying to figure out what to tell me. He thinks for a while and finally says, "Not really, Lu. Cameron tried to kill himself yesterday."

141

It's like a wave of frigid water hits me in the face, and suddenly I'm drowning in self-hatred. Yesterday? I ignored his messages! I should have read them. I should have answered him. I could have stopped him. I could have said something. I could have told someone. I could have done something. I was too busy worrying about myself to realize that he needed me.

"He's going to be all right," says Dad, answering the question before I ask it, "but he's in the hospital now. He'll be there for a while."

Cameron's been my friend since the day they brought me home from the hospital, his chubby little face right next to mine in every photo. He taught me to cuss, he taught me to rhyme, and he taught me to be proud of who I am. I can see him standing in my room right now in his tight, black jeans, his flannel shirt hanging down to his knees and his long brown hair tied back in a ponytail, reciting Shakespeare. Even when the words are confusing, he has a way of making me understand what they mean just with his face, and his tone of voice. I wasn't there for him when he

needed me most. I was too busy being selfish. I'm
crying now, giant silent tears.

"Honey," says Dad, putting his arm around me,
"it's okay. He'll be okay. Your Aunt is a mess, though,
and your mom is looking after her."

"Can I see him?"

"Not yet. But I'll find out when you can."

Going back to my room, I switch on my phone. I
never read his last two messages. Tears run down my
face as I open the first, which says:

> *You are tired*
> *(I think)*
> *Of the always puzzle of living and doing;*
> *And so am I.*

> *Come with me then*
> *And we'll leave it far and far away –*
> *(Only you and I understand!)*

It doesn't rhyme, and it doesn't even look like
poetry, but it's moving and beautiful anyway. The

second message is, I think, the next two stanzas of the poem:

> *You have played*
>
> *(I think)*
>
> *And broke the toys you were fondest of*
>
> *And are a little tired now;*
>
> *Tired of things that break and –*
>
> *Just tired.*

> *So am I.*

I should have read this yesterday! I would have known something was wrong. I could have done something.

I look up the lines and find out the poem is by e e cummings, who sometimes wrote his name in lower case letters like that. He wasn't all about rhyming; he liked to play with words and the order of words, and he tried to paint pictures with them that make you feel things. I think that's what Cam was doing, using the poems to paint a picture of his feelings. To tell me something without really telling me.

The Sign Around My Neck

I've managed to stop crying by the time I'm dressed and ready. Dad's made scrambled eggs and bacon for breakfast, which is unusual for a weekday. He sips his coffee and looks at me across the table. "I need to take you shopping," he announces, which is another crazy thing. "Those clothes don't look right on you anymore."

I'm wearing a navy blue girls' button-down shirt. It's got blue buttons that stop a few inches below my neck and sleeves that are sewn into cuffs high up on my arms. I hate it, but it's one of the least awful shirts I have.

"What about Mom?" I ask. "She's always the one who does that."

"I'll talk to her. Not right away, though. I'm sure she's upset about Cameron. Maybe we need to give her a break for a few days?"

"Yeah. That makes sense."

***

Dad drops me off at school, and I find Maddie sitting on a bench, checking her notifications. She takes

145

one look at me and immediately asks, "What happened?"

"Too much," I say, not knowing where to begin. "My mom didn't come home last night, and I know she was angry when she left."

"Did your parents have a fight?" Maddie's holding her breath in shock.

"Sort of. But that's not why she stayed at my Aunt Caroline's house." She relaxes. "Cam tried to kill himself yesterday. He's only fifteen, Maddie."

"Oh!" she gasps, her face suddenly sad. "That's horrible! Poor Cameron. Is he okay?"

"I guess so. He's in the hospital. I just. . . it's really messed up. He's been getting beat up at school. You know how he is, right?"

"Totally," she smiles. "He's one of a kind. I remember when he acted out that scene from *Romeo and Juliet* for us."

"Yeah," I laugh, "and when he put my mom's blouse on his head to be Juliet, I was laughing so hard, my stomach hurt." I pause. "He knows the whole play by heart, Mads. Every line."

"Wow." She thinks a minute and says, "I know what you mean, though. He's kind of weird and nerdy. And he's into girl stuff, like makeup and nail polish."

"It gets him in trouble." I kick at the dirt under my feet, not knowing what to do with all this anger and sadness. "My dad says he'll be okay, but it feels like something's broken now. I should have known, Mads. I think he was trying to tell me. I should have done something."

Ben and Asher walk up, and I drop the conversation. Ben's at least a foot taller than Asher and almost twice as wide. He's got his arm hanging over him in a way that says, "Don't mess with him because I've got his back," and Asher looks pretty happy about it.

"You want to come hang out on Saturday?" Ben's asking all of us. "My mom put up a zip line in the yard."

"Holy cow!" says Asher. "My mom would never let me have one of those."

"That's what happens when your parents are divorced," says Ben. "I think she feels guilty so she keeps buying me stuff."

"Your dad moved away, didn't he?" Asher looks embarrassed to mention it.

"Yeah, but that's just for work. It would have happened anyway. We're still really tight. We're all sharing a hotel room in Chicago for the wedding."

"Really?" asks Maddie. "Your parents are divorced, and they're still sharing a room?"

"Are you kidding?" laughs Ben. "They get along better now than they did when they were married!" I wonder if that's going to be true about my parents, too. They're already fighting over me. What if it gets worse?

I'm sitting in the doctor's office between Mom and Dad. They haven't been talking to each other much for the last few days. Mom's been spending a lot of time with Aunt Caroline while Cameron's in the hospital. They said I'm too young to visit him, so I made him a card instead. Inside, I wrote a poem:

I know you're feeling sad and tired,

but I want you to be inspired

to heal yourself and get home fast

so I can see your face at last

and say, "Don't hurt yourself again

'cause I need you around, my friend."

149

Mom's reading a parenting magazine, and Dad's looking at his phone. I'd be doing the same thing if I weren't so interested in all the posters on the walls. One says, "Feeling Upset? Here's 5 Ideas to Help with Anxiety," and shows five little animals doing things like exercising and eating healthy food. Another says, "What You Say in Here, Stays in Here," only there's a list of exceptions, like if someone is hurting you or you want to hurt someone else. There's a picture of a dog that says, "If You're Always Chasing Your Tail, The View Never Changes. Try Something New," and one of a cartoon brain inside a head that reads, "Don't Believe Everything You Think." That one actually makes me feel worse than I already do. Does it mean I shouldn't trust myself?

A man shows us into the doctor's office, and we all sit down across the desk from her. She looks familiar, but I'm not sure from where.

"Hello, Lu," she says. "It's nice to see you!" Suddenly I remember who she is.

"Hi, Ms. Perez!" I look at my parents. "She's Valentina's mom!"

"Hello Dr. Perez," says my Mom. "It's a pleasure to meet you. Lucy's told me what a talented gymnast your daughter is."

"Small world," says my Dad, reaching across the desk to shake her hand. "Good to meet you, doctor."

"Thank you," says Dr. Perez, "she works very hard at it. Of course I'm the one getting up at four AM to drive her to meets, but it's worth it." She turns to me. "So why are you all here today?" I'm waiting for Mom or Dad to say something but Valentina's mom is looking right at me.

"Because I'm a boy," I say at last.

"Oh?"

"Yes."

"I see. Well, I'll tell you what I'd like to do, Lu, if it's okay with you. Do you think you and I could talk alone for a little while? Then afterwards I'd like to see your mom and dad alone. What do you think? Does that sound all right to you?" Mom and Dad both seem fine with it so I nod. "Great. Okay then. Would you two mind waiting for us outside? It won't be long." They leave the room and I relax into the back of my chair.

"So," says Valentina's mom, "when did you decide that you're a boy?"

"I didn't 'decide' anything. I *am* a boy. It's just, my body's wrong. For a long time I thought it was my head that was wrong but now I know it's not."

"I see. And when did you start feeling this way?"

"I've *always* felt this way, for as long as I can remember."

"What do you think it means to be a boy?"

"I don't know. I guess you like boy things."

"Like what?"

"I don't mean sports, or anything. My dad doesn't even like sports."

"He doesn't?"

"No. He's more into old movies."

"What are you into?"

The Sign Around My Neck

"I like old movies, too. And music, and poetry. And science."

"Those don't sound like boy things to me."

"No, but . . . it's not about that. It's hard to explain."

"Can you try?"

I think as hard as I can but it's just too difficult to put into words. Feelings don't have words, sometimes. When I write a poem, if I can't say what they are, I explain what they're like. I use a simile to compare them to something else.

"It's like, when you're born, they hang a sign around your neck. And everybody reads that sign, and because of it they treat you a certain way and they expect you to act a certain way. And you're supposed to be into it. You're supposed to be happy about it. But you're not. It never feels right. It feels awful. And it just gets worse and worse every day. You look in the mirror, and it's just so clear to you that you got the wrong sign, but it doesn't matter because you're stuck

153

with it forever and there's nothing you can do about it. And you just want to, I don't know. Maybe give up."

"Okay. I think I understand."

Dr. Perez asks me if I feel safe at home. I tell her yes, totally, but Mom and Dad are fighting about me, and I'm worried they're going to get a divorce. When she asks me about school, I tell her there are bullies who pick on lots of kids, not just me.

"How about you, though? How do they make you feel?"

"Angry."

"Anything else?" she asks, eyebrows raised.

"Sad. Like it's never going to get better. Even if they stop picking on me, I'm still going to feel wrong inside."

Eventually she says, "All right, Lu, I think we're good," and sends me out to get my parents. They leave me in the waiting room and close the door so I can't hear them talking. It seems like they're in there forever before they finally come out. Dad shakes the doctor's hand again, then puts his arm around Mom.

"Thanks very much, Dr. Perez. We appreciate it."

"You're welcome. I encourage you both to think about what I said."

We get in the car to drive home. Mom turns on the radio, which is her way of saying she doesn't want to talk. She looks sad and angry, like me. I feel like I've let her down and I hate myself for it.

"Want to stop for a burger?" asks Dad.

"No, thanks," I say. I don't feel like eating.

"You sure? It's way past dinner time."

"Yeah."

"Well, I'm going through the drive-thru for me. Nicole?" Mom just shakes her head. "All right, then. Suit yourselves."

Dad eats his burger in the car while he's driving, and Mom yells at him to "Just pull over and eat!" He finishes it in about two bites, though, so it's pointless. When we get home, I go straight upstairs to my room and shut the door. I put on my headphones and lay down on the bed, letting the music sink into me.

I'm sitting down to dinner with Mom and Dad and Great-Great-Great-Grandma Anna is serving us. She's wearing the same dress from the photo, only that was sepia and the dress is actually blue. She's buttoned up all the way to her chin and down to her wrists. She keeps calling us "*My dah-links*" in a funny accent and putting food on our plates. No matter how much we eat, she brings us more. We start with a giant stuffed turkey and a tray of lasagna. When she carries out a baked ham, Dad says, "I thought you kept kosher?" and she tells him, "We left that behind in the Old Country, *dah-link*. Eat, there's more." Plates upon plates of food are on the table, more than the three of us could eat in a year. There are candied yams and twice-baked potatoes; three kinds of stuffing and cornbread with gravy; fried chicken and French fries; hotdogs and hamburgers; burritos, enchiladas, and tacos; pad Thai, pork fried rice, barbequed spare ribs, and dozens of different sushi rolls; meatballs, sausage, and salami; and heaps of pies, cookies, and cakes. Grandma brings out dish after dish as the table expands to hold it all.

Mom and Dad are eating and laughing and having a wonderful time, but something feels wrong. Grandma Anna is saying, "Eat, *dah-link*, eat!" but I can't reach any of the food. I'm stretching myself out across the table but the plates just get further away from me. She's looking at me like her feelings are hurt, and she can't understand why I'm not eating. I try to explain, but she can't hear me over the noise of the dishes and the chewing. Her eyes get sadder and sadder and she starts crying. She's pleading, "Eat, *dah-link*, eat!" and I want to, but the food won't let me

157

touch it. Dad shakes his head and says, "She did all of this for you. The least you can do is enjoy it."

My alarm goes off, and I wake up with a clear memory of the dream. At first I'm confused; I think Grandma Anna must be in the house somewhere. Then I remember that she died a very long time ago. It's a strange feeling, though, as if she were just in the room with me. Was she visiting me? I go over the details in my head. Grandma Anna made a feast for us, and I was the only one who couldn't enjoy it. It was right there in front of me, a giant gift from her, and I couldn't get to any of it. What was she trying to tell me?

"Just find your stance," says Ben. I'm standing on his skateboard on the lawn in front of his house. There's a dad tossing a baseball to his daughter across the street. She's maybe four years old, and the bat is definitely too big for her. Her curly red hair frames her determined little face as she swings and nearly falls over. She keeps looking at me like I'm nuts.

"Why are we in the grass?" I ask. "Shouldn't we be on the sidewalk?"

"Not unless you want to get hurt! You need to get comfortable on the board first. This way, you won't roll away."

"Like this?" I ask, trying to place my feet on the board exactly how he showed me.

"Yeah. Make sure your front foot is over the trucks."

"The trucks?"

"The wheels."

"Right."

"Try bending your knees and bouncing up and down a bit, just to get the feel of it." I do as he says. "Now switch feet. Put the other one in front. We need to see if you ride goofy."

"I'm going to look goofy no matter what, Ben. I have no idea what I'm doing."

"Dude. 'Goofy' means you lead with your right foot and push with your left. Most people do it the other way."

"Oh. Good to know."

Ben makes me stand on the board in the grass for a while before he hands me his helmet and points at his driveway. It's nice and flat. "Go practice there," he says. "The same thing."

"Just standing on it?"

"Balancing. Getting comfortable. Shifting your weight from one set of trucks to the other."

I bend down to pick up the board and hear a loud CRACK! When I turn around to see where it came from, Ben is lying on the ground. The dad from across the street runs over, and I realize Ben's been hit by the baseball.

"Ben!" I run to his side and kneel down. He's not bleeding anywhere but there's already a huge bump on the side of his head. "Are you okay?"

"I think so," he says slowly. "I'm not sure."

"Did I hurt him, Daddy?" The little girl looks like she's about to cry.

"It's okay, sweetie. It was an accident. You didn't mean to." She starts bawling like kids do, wailing like a horrible siren with her mouth wide open.

"Please," the man says to me, "can you go get his mother?" He turns back to Ben. "I'm sorry, Ben. I never expected her to whack the ball like that." The kid screams and wails even louder.

161

"It's okay, Grace. He'll be all right."

Ben starts to get up but drops back to the grass. "I feel weird."

I run into Ben's house calling out for his mom, and she comes up from the basement with a basket full of laundry.

"What's wrong, Lu?"

"I think he's okay but Ben got hit in the head with a baseball." I learned from Dad to lead with the good news.

She drops the laundry basket where she's standing and runs outside.

"Baby," she says, kneeling over him, "are you all right?"

"I'm not sure. I feel kind of funny." They help him to his feet and into the house where he lies down on the couch. The man's got his daughter in his arms and he can't stop apologizing. Ben's mom calls the doctor.

"Come on," she says, hanging up the phone. "We're taking you for an X-ray. I'll drop you off at home, Lu." She turns to the man from across the street.

"It's okay, Matt. Why don't you take Grace home? I'll talk to you later."

She drops me off in front of my house, and I make Ben promise to message me later. Mom and Dad are upstairs in their bedroom, so they don't hear me come in. I can hear them, though, and they're talking about Cameron.

"He's going to be all right, Nicole." Dad's voice has a tone in it that tells me Mom is crying.

"How do you know, Dan? How do you know he's going to be all right? How do you know the bullying is going to stop?" She sounds angry, but not at Dad.

"I don't. But at least we all know what's going on now. We can give him the help he needs."

"I don't know what I'd do, Dan."

"About what?" There's a long pause and then Dad says, "It's Lu you're worried about, isn't it?"

"What if she gets bullied like Cameron?"

"You heard what the doctor said, honey. It'll be worse if we force him to be someone he's not."

163

"I know," she says, about as sad as I've ever heard her. "I know."

I'm wearing my favorite outfit: My Dad's brown belt and the green checked shirt. It's the only thing I feel like myself in, but it disappeared for a while when Mom washed it. I was happy to see it hanging in my closet again this morning. I wonder if it has anything to do with what Dr. Perez said.

We're rehearsing the play, and I'm doing all the mom's lines in the funny voice without *being* her. I tell myself I'm just imitating her. When the scene is over, we break for lunch, and Ms. Baxter says she's going to be fitting our costumes. The play is in just a few days. When she calls my name, I step inside the dressing room she's made by putting a curtain on a hula hoop and hanging it from a light stand. She hands my costumes to me through the curtain.

I start with the bartender's outfit. The black pants are a little too big but Ms. Baxter says they'll be fine with a belt. The vest is red brocade, woven throughout with golden thread in a delicate repeating pattern. I put it on, and she spins me around to place a few pins into the back so she can alter it to fit me later. The shirt fits fine, but the sleeves are too long, so she rolls them into cuffs for me. Next comes the bandleader from the '40s. He's got the same pants and shirt, but they go with a white bow tie and jacket. We don't put the bow tie on, but she has me try the jacket, and I love the way it feels. It's heavy on my shoulders but soft to the touch. Next up is the ugly dress.

"Can I put it on over this?" I ask, pointing at the shirt and pants. I'm going to feel naked in that thing.

"Don't be silly, Lu. Go on now, I've got a lot of costumes to get through."

Inside the tiny fabric room, I begin to undress. The hair on my arms stands up as my eyes begin to water. I blink, determined not to cry. I don't want anyone to see me in this dress, but there's nothing I can do about it. The boys are going to make fun of me no matter what, in the dress or out of it. There's no way I can win. I'm completely trapped. The misery takes me. I try to think of the beach – of the sand, the wind, and the waves – but it's too late. I must be in there too long because Ms. Baxter pokes her head in and sees me huddled on the floor, crying silently.

"Oh, for goodness sake!" She puts her hand on my back. "Go on, get dressed, Lu. I'm sure the dress will fit you fine." When I emerge, she takes my hand. "It's not a big deal. It's just a costume for a play and you're an actor. This is what they wore back then." She pauses for a moment, thinking. "I'm sorry you don't like the dress. Do you want to wear one of the other ones?"

"No. It's fine." I can't bear the thought of trying on *any* dress.

"All right. Go wash your face and drink some water."

Maddie follows me out to the girls' room. I hesitate for a second before going in because it feels so wrong. I don't have a choice. She walks in after me and the door closes behind us.

"What's wrong, Lu? Are you okay?"

"Yeah," I say, clenching my fists. "It's just that dress. I can't handle it."

"She shouldn't make you wear it. She should let you wear jeans just like the protesters."

"She doesn't understand how I feel." I let myself relax and fall back against a wall.

"Can't you explain it?"

"I don't even understand it myself, Maddie."

"Then what are you going to do?"

"I don't know. Dad says the costumes are up to her. She's the director."

"Well," she says, frowning, "you could quit the play."

"I don't want to. It's fun. Why should I have to give it up? Plus, I'm not a quitter."

"Then you're kind of stuck, aren't you?"

"Yeah." I'm getting used to the feeling.

Mom's working late again tonight, so Dad and I are having dinner alone. He's ordered a pizza because he knows I'm tired of ham sandwiches. I tell him about the dream I had with Great-Great-Great-Grandma Anna.

"Some people think that your ancestors do come to visit in your dreams," he says, "to let you know they're still watching over you. Others believe that everyone in your dream is just a part of yourself."

"What do you think?"

"I think it depends on the dream. What do you think?"

"I think Grandma Anna was really there. She seemed so real. I could smell her perfume. And when I woke up, it was like she was still in the room with me." Dad looks at me like he's seriously considering it.

"Then maybe she was," he says, taking a bite of his pizza. "What do you think she was trying to tell you?"

"I don't know. There was so much food! All kinds of stuff, like turkey and lasagna and sushi."

"That's quite an international buffet."

"She was crying because I wasn't eating. You were upset, too. You said she'd made it all just for me."

"Ah, that makes sense."

"It does?"

"Sure. All that food on the table? That represents America, full of people from all over the world. Grandma gave you America."

"Then why couldn't I eat anything?"

"You tell me, Kiddo."

"I don't know."

"Think about it. What did she give you by coming to America? Besides all of that food?" Mom's words

171

ring in my ears. *You have the right to be exactly who you are.*

"The right to be myself?"

"And are you doing that?"

"No. Not yet."

"Well there you go. Makes perfect sense to me. Grandma wants you to be happy."

It's checked shirt day again. I know I wore it yesterday, but I don't care. Mom has stopped making a fuss about it. When she sees me walk into the kitchen, she just sighs and says, "Good morning, Honey." I've got my hair pulled back into a tight ponytail, so if you saw me from the front, you'd think I'm a boy. It's the best I know how to feel, and my day is going great so far. My project on photosynthesis made it into the science fair and I got an "A" on my Western Expansion essay. Ben messaged me to say he's feeling better and he'll be back at school tomorrow. Cam's coming home from the hospital this weekend, and Dad called me "Son" when he dropped me off at school this morning.

Maddie and I are on our way to lunch when I stop to use the restroom. I'm standing outside the girls' room door, and I think about Grandma Anna and what Mom and Dad have said: I have the right to be myself. Grandma Anna gave me that right, and she wants me to use it. She risked her life for it. I take a deep breath and walk into the boys' room as I hear Maddie gasp behind me.

I walk in and thankfully, it's empty. I go into a stall and just as I'm sitting down, I hear two boys come in. Just my luck! It's Sam and Noah.

"It's cool," says Sam. "I didn't care. I stayed in my room and played video games."

"Wow," says Noah, plainly jealous. "I wish I got suspended from school!" I feel a sneeze coming on. I clamp my nose shut with my fingers and hold my hands over my face.

"No, you don't. I have a week of school I have to make up over summer break. It totally sucks. Now I

174

can't go away to camp and I have to stay home with my lousy stepdad. He's a total jerk."

"Doesn't he work?"

"Yeah. He works at drinking!" They both laugh. That's when I sneeze. It's muffled, but they hear it.

"Who's in there?" says Noah. The next thing I know, he's peeking under the door at me. "Holy cow, it's Big Bertha! What are *you* doing in here?"

"You're kidding!" says Sam, and I can hear the excitement in his voice. They both begin pulling and shaking the door until they get it open, which isn't hard because the lock barely works. The grab me by my arms and pull me out of the stall.

"What's *wrong* with you?" Sam's face is red with rage. "First you jump me, now you're in *here*? You think you're a boy, don't you?"

"Yeah," adds Noah, tightening his grip on my arm, "you're a total freak! Check out her shirt, Sam. I bet she got it in the boys' department."

"Nice shirt!" says Sam, and I know it's not a compliment. "Let's get it off her!"

175

I panic and start fighting back with all my strength. I'm bigger than both of them, but it's two against one. Cowards! They're too scared to take me on alone but together, they think they're tough. We're rolling around on the floor and I'm throwing punches but none of them hits anything. Now they've got me on my back and they're both on top on me. If only Ben were here, I know he'd pull them off me. I'm struggling and screaming, I can't do anything to make them stop, and I'm running out of breath and energy. Noah's holding me down and Sam's almost got my shirt off. Suddenly Noah screams, and then Sam. They both jump off me like they're on fire and start wildly beating themselves. I look up and see Maddie standing there, holding an empty hamster pouch. She's put mice down their backs!

"Come on," she says, helping me get up, "let's get out of here!" She pulls me out of the restroom and half way down the hall before I remember the mice.

"What about your mice?"

"Whatever. You're more important."

"I thought we said we were going to take things slowly?" Dad looks like he's more worried than disappointed, but Mom looks angry.

"I thought we said I have the right to be who I am," I say softly.

"At any rate," says Dr. Petersen, "if this is Lu's choice, then we need to discuss it. I'm not sure the school is prepared to deal with it."

"It's not a choice," says Dad. "It's who he is."

"Have you consulted a doctor?"

"Of course we have," says Dad, losing patience.

Mom is so very quiet.

"Well, the school year is almost over. Perhaps next year we can set up a plan to – "

"No," says Mom, rising from her chair. I can almost see the steam coming out of her ears. "Here's what's going to happen. You're going to take that staff restroom, the one with only one stall in it, and you're going to make it a gender inclusive restroom. Which means that anyone can use it, one person at a time. And you're going to do it before the end of the day today, or I'll be filing a lawsuit against you, the school, and the district for willfully endangering the welfare of my child in a manner that already constitutes harassment. And you'll find, Dr. Petersen, if you look me up, that I'm rather well known for winning cases just like this one. So I need you to listen carefully to what I'm saying here: You WILL keep my child safe in this school. Am I understood?"

Dr. Petersen looks like someone is pointing a gun at him, and he'd do anything to make them drop it.

"Please now, let's stay calm!" This makes Mom even angrier.

"Oh, no you don't," she starts, and I know what's coming. "You do NOT tell a woman whose child has just been assaulted to CALM DOWN. You FIX the PROBLEM." She takes me by the hand and looks at Dad. "I've said what I came to say, Dan. Let's go." I'm not sure what it all means, but I know it's good!

We get in the car and Dad starts the engine.

"You've won cases just like this one?" he asks, as surprised as I am.

"Of course not. Let's go get a burger."

Maddie and I are standing in the schoolyard, waiting for the morning bell to ring. Her phone is buzzing with messages somewhere inside the purple backpack at her feet, but she doesn't seem to care.

"So how's it going?" she asks.

"Okay, I guess."

"What about your mom?"

"She's definitely not ready to call me her son yet. But she gets it that I'm not changing, and I know she loves me anyway. You should have heard her telling off Dr. P.! *'You WILL keep my child safe in this school!'* It was awesome." Ben walks over and raises his eyebrows at Maddie.

"I heard you kicked some butt yesterday." He smiles at her like he's proud and impressed. We both know it was all over the school about two minutes after it happened.

"Yeah, well. I was just thinking fast." Now that the moment has passed, I can see that she's sad about her mice. I put my hand on her shoulder.

"Didn't Asher tell you?"

"Tell me what?"

"He has your mice." Maddie looks stunned.

"You're kidding! How?"

"I messaged him while I was waiting for my parents. He got the new science teacher to help him catch them before they got out of the boys' room."

"Oh my gosh, Lu, that's awesome! You're wonderful!" She throws her arms around me and gives me a giant kiss on the cheek. She's been my best friend for years, but I blush.

181

"So," says Ben, once Maddie has finished doing a small dance of joy, "did you hear that Sam and Noah got suspended for the rest of the year? They'll both be in school all summer." A huge smile settles on my face.

"Serves them right," says Maddie, "beating up on my mice!" and we all laugh.

When Asher shows up, he hands Maddie a plastic container with air holes on top and two mice inside. She pulls the hamster pouch out of her backpack and returns them safely to their home.

"Are you going to hide them from your Mom forever?" I ask.

"Probably. Unless I can keep them at your house?"

"I'll ask my mom."

The bell rings and we all file into school. As we walk down the hallway to Mrs. Rubin's class, we go right past the teacher's restroom – only now the sign says "STUDENT RESTROOM," and it's got the stick figure man *and* the triangle woman on it. Way to go, Mom!

I knock on Cam's door, and it takes him a minute
to answer, but he tells me to come in. The room is a
jumble of books and posters, calendars and cards taped
to every inch of available wall, a riot of color and
motion in each image, taken, I think, from dozens of
plays and musicals. I recognize scenes from *Wicked* and
several other shows, but the centerpiece of the room is
a framed poster of *Romeo and Juliet* from a production
by the Royal Shakespeare Company in England. It
holds a place of honor directly opposite his pillow
where it's the first thing he sees each morning and the
last thing he sees at night. He's propped up in bed with
a book in his hands: *The Complete Works of William*

Shakespeare. Like curtains on a stage, brick red drapes are drawn against the insistent sun of early June, a lone ray passing between them to cast a triangle of light across the pages.

"Hey," I say, unsure where to begin. There's so much I want to tell him.

"Hey." He smiles weakly as he looks up from his book.

"I'm glad you're home." Sitting down on the foot of his bed, I realize he looks different. Normally he's totally put together, from his lace-up boots to his skinny jeans and eyeliner; today he's wearing sweatpants and a hoodie. No make-up. No nail polish. I can't tell yet if he's super sad or just really relaxed. "I missed you."

"Yeah," he frowns. "Me too." Closing the book, he sets it on his nightstand as if it were made of glass. "I hated being in the hospital."

"I'm sorry." I think about him there all alone, seeing it in my mind as a long gray corridor of peeling paint and narrow doorways, wanting to come home but afraid of going back to school, of facing his mom and maybe even me. A million miserable feelings flow from my heart to my head and straight out of my eyes as tears, which I don't want. I can't control them any more than the words that come spilling out of me.

"I'm sorry I didn't answer your messages, Cam. It's all my fault. I feel terrible. I should have been there for you. This wouldn't have happened."

"What are you talking about, Lu? That's crazy!" He folds his legs up so he can lean in close and puts his hand on my shoulder. "Why would you think that?"

"The poems," I sob, wiping snot away with my sleeve. "e e cummings. I should have read them when you sent them. I would have known something was wrong. I would have done something. I was too busy feeling sorry for myself to even look at them." He gets up from his bed and leaves the room but comes right back with a box of tissues and hands it to me. Sitting down, he waits for me to stop blowing my nose before speaking.

"Lu, I'm the only one who's responsible for what I did. It's not your job to take care of me. Geez," he snorts, a little angry with himself, "I'm the older one. I should be looking after you." After a minute, he asks, "Why were you feeling sorry for yourself?"

"You first," I insist, and immediately stop crying. "What happened?"

"They didn't tell you?" He seems surprised.

"Well, yeah. They said you tried to kill yourself."

"Not exactly." Biting his lower lip, he looks down at the bed. "Although I guess it looked that way." He scratches at his chin, where dark wispy hairs are starting to poke through. Sighing deeply, his whole body heaves with the breath. "I didn't want to die, Lu. I just wanted to. . . I don't know. Escape? I needed to stop thinking long enough to be able to rest. I couldn't turn my brain off, replaying stuff over and over again, all the time. The locker room. The lunch room. The alley behind the school. Everywhere, every time they'd ever laid a hand on me. I couldn't stop being afraid."

"Geez, Cam, I'm so sorry. That sounds awful."

"It was. So I drank a bottle of cold medicine. Not the whole thing, but whatever was left in it. I just wanted to sleep, Lu. I was so tired of fighting." He looks tired just talking about it, but now he's made me angry.

"That was really stupid, Cam." I want to tell him off. He needs to know how selfish he was, how much he hurt his mom and mine, and me, and how much worse and horrible and permanent it could have been. But the last thing I want to do right now is have a fight with him, so I bite my tongue and file it away for another time.

"I know," he nods sadly. "I just. . . I didn't see any other way."

"So what happened to you?" I imagine Aunt Caroline finding him passed out on the floor, almost dead, and I want to punch him.

"I thought I'd fall asleep and that would be it, but no. I got sick enough to where I really felt like I was dying. Throwing up, stomach pain like a million knives. Nothing's ever hurt so bad in all my life. I

187

blacked out, and Mom called an ambulance. The next thing I know, I'm waking up in a hospital, and they won't let me leave until I convince them that I won't go home and do it again. Believe me, Lu, I'd *never* be dumb enough to do it again. I'm sorry you feel responsible, but it didn't have anything to do with you."

"I'm glad you didn't want to die, Cam." As glad as I am that he's okay, part of me is glad he paid a price for being so stupid. "I'm sorry it hurt you," I offer, only half meaning it. "It hurt us, too."

"I know," he admits. "I'm sorry."

"So what happens next?"

"I have to see a therapist and a doctor who checks in on me." Cam makes a face that says he thinks it's a waste of time.

"Do they help?" I'm playing with a ring on my fourth finger, spinning it around with my thumb to keep from exploding at him.

"*Everyone can master a grief but he that has it,*" he says, his expression turning serious.

188

"Shakespeare?" I'm spinning the ring, forwards and back, forwards and back.

"Of course," he confirms, "from *Much Ado about Nothing*. It means: it's easy to tell someone how to feel when you're not the one with the sorrow."

I know he's not talking about me, but it hits me square in the throat. He's right: I have no idea what he was feeling. My anger fades away as he folds his hands between his knees and stares down at the floor, trying to think of something positive to say. Finally, he looks up at me.

"They do their best, I think. They explained to me that my reaction wasn't so crazy, considering what was going on. They said I was 'traumatized' by a bunch of really bad experiences, so I reacted by shutting down, which I guess is kind of normal. So I feel a little better about that. Now I know I have other options. I don't have to let things get so bad before asking for help."

"That's good," I nod, happy to hear some confidence creep into his voice. "But what about school?"

"That's the good part!" Suddenly a smile lights up his face. "I don't have to go back!"

"Really? What are you going to do?"

"Mom says I can do school online, as long as I get out of the house and spend time with people on a regular basis. So I'm joining the Young People's Shakespeare Company and performing for kids!" A lightness has entered his body and lifted up his chin, and it dawns on me that he looks a bit like the Romeo in his poster – full of hope and excitement.

"No way! That's awesome! It's perfect for you."

"Yeah, I know! That's why I'm reading this." He nods toward the book. "I want to be ready for my first audition."

"That's great, Cam. I'm really happy for you." And I am, because it seems like the perfect solution.

"Now it's your turn," he says with his eyebrows raised. "What was going on with you that night? Why were you feeling sorry for yourself?"

I sigh deeply and begin to stare at my feet. It feels like too much to explain. I'm not sure I want to ask him to deal with it right now with everything else he's been through. It feels like a few minutes go by before he smiles and shakes his head at me.

"Ah, my dear Lu!" Cam exclaims, thrusting his finger in the air. "*This above all: to thine own self be true. Dude knew what he was talking about.*"

"What do you mean?" I ask, startled to think he might already know my secret.

"I'm saying, my dear cousin, that I know you are my brother."

How is that even possible? Does he have special powers? My jaw must be on the floor, but he just laughs and ruffles my hair.

"How?" I manage, as if shock and joy have together agreed to cut off the rest of my words.

"You know I want to be an actor, right? Well, actors study people, and one thing that's clear is that guys and girls have totally different body language. I've known you since you were born, and you've always been more 'guy' to me. Lately you seem more comfortable with it, like really happy in your 'guy'-

191

ness, or whatever. It feels like you're ready to own it and just be who you are. It's cool. I'm proud of you. I don't want you to suffer. Those poems I sent you – the lines from e e cummings and all of the others – they were about you, too, you know. I think we both were tired '*of the always puzzle of living and doing*' - of pretending things were okay." I let his words sink in.

"I can't believe you, Cam. I love you."

"I love you too." He gives me a quick hug and then looks me in the eye. "Now it's time for both of us to heal and move forward."

It's show time. Mom's busy in the bedroom with the door closed. Dad says she's running late, so he drops me off backstage and goes out to save them seats in the theater. I have no idea how I'm going to get through the play because all I can think about is that horrible dress. I put on the bartender costume and try to get my mind to focus on something else. The beach. The sand. The waves. Ms. Baxter calls "Places!" and everyone in the first scene goes out to their assigned spots on stage. The lights go down and the curtain rises.

A group of students are walking through a costume shop like the one that Ms. Baxter's family owns. Set up on stage are kids who are playing mannequins, each dressed in an outfit that represents a different part of the 20th century. The students thank the shop's manager and say goodbye. She locks up and follows them out. Two kids walk out on stage; they realize they've been locked in by accident.

The music starts, and all the mannequins come to life to explain to the kids that they're going on a trip through history. It's a huge scene and everyone is in it, so I get to be on stage. I can see Dad in the third row, but Mom's not there yet. I can't believe she's late. Even if she doesn't want to see me play a boy onstage, I'm pretty sure she'd like to see me in a dress. In a way, I understand that. She's still attached to the daughter she thought she had.

A couple of scenes later, I take my place on stage as the bartender, and I'm totally distracted. Mom's still not here and I still have to put on that dress. I still have to live out my nightmare in front of the entire school.

Two more scenes go by, and I'm on stage again as the bandleader and nothing has changed except that I'm ten minutes closer to doom.

I'm sweating when I walk off the stage this time because I know I have to put on the dress. There's no escaping it. As I work through my thoughts, I can't help but rhyme them:

> *I can hear my own thundering heartbeat.*
> *My hands are freezing cold.*
> *Part of me feels like I'm floating away,*
> *and part of me wants to explode.*

I'm losing myself in the rhythm of the rhyme, closing my eyes and riding on a cloud of beats and words and –

"Lu!" A voice snaps me back to reality. "Lu!" I turn around, and it's Mom. "Wait right there!" She says something quickly to Ms. Baxter and then runs over to me with a plastic shopping bag in her hands.

"Hurry," she says, "put these on." Reaching into the bag, she pulls out Grandma Sarah's jeans, complete with the giant peace-sign patches! "I'm sorry I got here so late, honey. Grandma sent them days ago, but they didn't arrive till today. I've been working all afternoon to make them fit you." I step into them and zip them up, and they fit perfectly!

"Wow, Mom, this is amazing! I can't believe it. Thank you so much!" Then I realize I'm still wearing the bandleader's shirt. "But what'll I wear on top?"

"Ha! I've already thought of that!" She pulls out a colorful short-sleeved shirt and shows it to me. "It's called a *dashiki*. Everyone wore these things in the '60s, both men and women." Relieved beyond words, I get it on just in time to run out on stage for the scene.

Mom, Dad, and I are sitting in a restaurant after the show; they say we're celebrating my "stellar performance." I figure it's probably the best time to ask them about the mice so I go for it, and I'm surprised by how quickly they agree. I don't really want them, but I owe it to Maddie, and they're kind of cute anyway.

"So," says Dad as they're both dipping their spoons into my sundae, "your mom and I have been talking. If you're going to be a boy, then you may want to change your name. Have you given any thought to it?" Mom is staring at her spoon and stirring her coffee slowly.

"Yes," I say, "I have."

"You have? So what do you think?"

"I think I want to keep my name. Mom gave it to me for her sister and I want to keep it." Mom looks up.

"You want to be a boy named Lucy?" she asks, looking completely confused.

"No. Lou."

"Lu?"

"As in Louie. Or Louis. I'd still be called 'Lu,' though." No one says anything for a while. "So what do you think?"

Mom eyes are wet with tears.

"I think it's just perfect, Honey."

"Dad?"

"Sounds good to me, Son." It's fine with me if he never calls me 'Honey' again, as long as he calls me that.

35

It's the first day of middle school, and things didn't go exactly as I planned. All the kids who knew me before are going to the same school that I am, so there's no fresh start after all. To them, I was a girl named Lu, but my friends know I've always been Lou inside. Now Lou is on the outside, too, and I don't know how everyone else will react. The school knows about me though, and they promised my parents I'd be safe. There are even other transgender students here!

My hair is shaved close at the sides and the back, and it's short enough on top to spike up with gel. Dad says I have his father's widow's peak, which is a weird thing to call a patch of hair. Mom took me shopping for all new clothes, and I got everything in the boys' department, even underwear. It doesn't matter that I'm the only one who knows I'm wearing them, it still makes a difference to me.

Dad helped me pick out my outfit this morning. I'm wearing a long-sleeved light blue shirt with tiny yellow ducks on it. The sleeves are rolled up past my elbows, and it's tucked into my jeans with a brand-new belt that matches the brown, lace-up shoes on my feet. I feel solid enough to face the world now.

Maddie's still my best friend, and she probably always will be. Things are only a little bit different now that she sees me as a guy. We don't go to the restroom together anymore, and we don't change in front of each other, but other than that, she treats me exactly the same. She's still trying to get me to spit water out of my nose when her mother isn't around. We're sitting on a bench outside our new school, ten minutes too early for homeroom.

"So what do you think?" Maddie asks. "Are you ready?"

"Yes." I think about what my parents have said, and about Dr. Perez's advice. I know I could be bullied for showing up to school looking like this, but it hardly matters to me. I was bullied before I cut my hair. It's a lose-lose situation, so I might as well be happy.

"Give me your schedule," she says, pulling out her own. "I want to see what classes we have together."

"What are you going to do, Mads? Follow me around with a pouch full of mice?" We both laugh but part of me is a little afraid. What if something bad happens?

Ben and Asher ride past us on their bikes and come over once they've locked them up. They both give me a fist bump and sit down.

"What are you doing?" asks Asher. Maddie explains that we're comparing our schedule so she can look after me – her words, not mine.

"That's a good idea," says Ben, pulling his schedule out of his backpack. He must have grown at least another three inches while he was away at baseball camp this summer.

"Look, you guys," I start, "this is really nice and all, but – "

"But you're happy to have them help you," says Asher, and I know he knows what he's talking about.

"Okay," I say, admitting it's not a bad idea to have some backup.

I'm peering over Maddie's shoulder at her schedule when I hear Ben say, "Hey, Dude!" and look up to see him high-fiving Jake Ruggiero. Suddenly I can feel my heart pounding in my chest. I'm afraid of what I might see in his face when he looks at me and realizes who I am.

"What's up, Ben?"

"Nothing much, Man. Baseball camp was the best. I'm sort of sad to be home."

"Yeah, me too," says Jake, kicking the dirt with his shoe. "That woman coach was amazing! She taught me more in two weeks than I learned all year on the team."

"I know, right? She was awesome." I didn't realize they'd been at baseball camp together.

"So what are you guys doing?" Jake asks, nodding toward the rest of us.

"Oh, we're just checking out Lou's schedule to see what classes we have with him. We're going to help him watch his back until he gets comfortable here."

"Cool," says Jake, pulling his schedule out of his back pocket. "Let me see what you've got, Lou." I hand mine to him. He looks at it for a minute, and then right at me. "Well, Dude," he says, "I've got you covered fourth period. Who's got fifth?"

Lucas Hasten

ACKNOWLEDGEMENTS

I would like to thank my big sister, Marla Schreibman, who has unfailingly embraced me with loving support from the moment I was born. She comes to me without the baggage of expectations beyond my own happiness, and she would stand before me as a shield against sorrow if she could. I owe much of what I accomplish to the guidance she has given me throughout my life.

This book is dedicated to my wife, Tessa Gaddis, who has stood solidly by my side since long before I began my transition from female to male. She is the inspiration and the motivation for this story because she told me I should write it. As a K-8 school librarian, it is her mission to "make sure that every kid sees themselves in the stacks," which she passionately stocks with volumes about children of every identity and ethnicity. When she brought home a handful of books about transgender kids for me to read, I found them depressing and difficult to relate to. That's when I resolved to write a story about a transgender boy who is reasonably happy and well-adjusted, with a circle of friends and parents who love him. It's the book I'd want to read if I were a kid.

I tried briefly to find a publisher for this book but decided to self-publish in order to release it as quickly as possible. I asked many people to read it before doing so and received invaluable feedback that caused me to extend and revise it substantially. Erica Bretall was instrumental in this regard; I might well have settled for a lesser work were I not almost embarrassed by her incisive critique. Heather Dubnick provided proofreading while Mary Spilsbury, Lane Robbins, June Palladino, Mona Alves, Karen Haber, El Sands, Dade Barlow, Arthur Petinsky, Sylvia Rupani-Smith, and Tara Colville all gave helpful feedback, as did their children and grandchildren.

Readers make snap decisions about whether or not to flip open a book based exclusively on its title and cover. One factor in my decision to self-publish was the knowledge that I could deliver an excellent cover thanks to the help of Lorna Gaddis. I am continually awed by the work she produces and grateful for her assistance with this project.

My parents, Shirley and Morton Hasten, are unfortunately long gone, but I cannot let this book out into the word without thanking them. They are in my thoughts every day. I know they would be proud of me.

About the Author

Lucas Hasten is a transgender man who spent an entire lifetime in the wrong body before realizing he could be in the right one. He lives happily in northern California with his wife and two small dogs, where he teaches, writes, and takes photographs. You can find him online at lucashasten.com.

Made in the USA
San Bernardino, CA
05 April 2018